the teeniest superhero

A MESSAGE FROM CHICKEN HOUSE

I'd love to welcome Milton back with open arms, but I don't have as many limbs as he does. Besides, he's become a bit of a handful since his first adventure in *Milton the Mighty* . . . But luckily his friends are here to bring him back to earth, despite some ghastly threats from humankind! Fun, friendship and concern for other living things are what makes Emma Read's series a Must Read!

BARRY CUNNINGHAM
Publisher
Chicken House

MILTON THE MEGASTAR

EMMA READ

Chicken House

2 Palmer Street, Frome, Somerset BA11 1DS
www.chickenhousebooks.com

Text © Emma Read 2020
Cover illustration © Alex G. Griffiths 2020
Interior illustrations © Lisa Reed 2020

First published in Great Britain in 2020
Chicken House
2 Palmer Street
Frome, Somerset BA11 1DS
United Kingdom
www.chickenhousebooks.com

Cover and interior design by Helen Crawford-White
Cover illustration by Alex G. Griffiths
Interior illustrations by Lisa Reed, in the style of Alex G. Griffiths

Typeset by Dorchester Typesetting Group Ltd
Printed and bound in Great Britain by CPI Group (UK) Ltd, Croydon CR0 4YY

The paper used in this Chicken House book is made from
wood grown in sustainable forests.

1 3 5 7 9 10 8 6 4 2

British Library Cataloguing in Publication data available.

PB ISBN 978-1-912626-06-9
eISBN 978-1-912626-92-2

To all the Spider Warriors

Also by Emma Read

Milton the Mighty

CHAPTER
1
Running and Flapping

'Milton said he would get the ladybird juice himself,' Audrey called, from the top of a rose bush.

'Careful up there!' said Ralph. 'That bunting's not worth being eaten by a bird over.'

'I'm fine. You concentrate on moving those benches and setting the tables. This must be the biggest charity fundraiser he's done yet – there's still loads to do.'

'At least he's mucking in this time. Not like the last—' Ralph stopped mid-sentence. 'Shh, here he comes.'

Milton scurried across the patio towards his

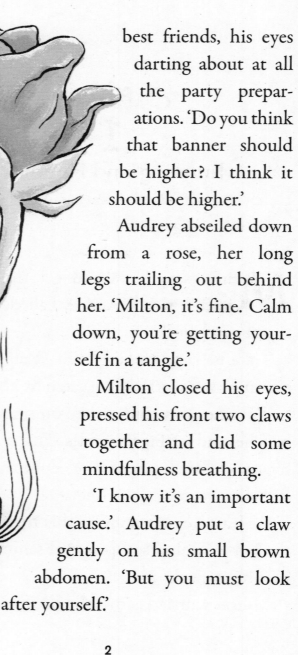

best friends, his eyes darting about at all the party preparations. 'Do you think that banner should be higher? I think it should be higher.'

Audrey abseiled down from a rose, her long legs trailing out behind her. 'Milton, it's fine. Calm down, you're getting yourself in a tangle.'

Milton closed his eyes, pressed his front two claws together and did some mindfulness breathing.

'I know it's an important cause.' Audrey put a claw gently on his small brown abdomen. 'But you must look after yourself.'

Milton glanced again at the banner, flapping gently in the early summer breeze.

BugKILL! Benefit Buffet

Six months had passed since the terror of last autumn, when Felicity Thrubwell and her company, BugKILL!, came to their road. She and her spider-hating exterminators had convinced the humans that Milton and his species of false widows were deadly, and she'd tried to kill them all. If it hadn't been for Milton and his BHF (best human friend), Zoe, creating the *#NotScaredOfSpiders* campaign, they would've all been wiped out. Spider-kind had been saved, but the effects of Felicity's reign of terror were still felt all over town. Everyone knew someone who had been affected by the BugKILL! disaster.

Milton looked at Audrey, who'd lost the sight in three of her eyes thanks to Felicity's pesticide spray, and sighed. There was still work to be done.

Despite her injury, Audrey always managed to pull off a perfect stern look. 'You're working too hard. Perhaps you should cut back on the public appearances.'

Milton was unmoved. 'Being a celebrity means hard work. I have to do what the campaign needs. Spiders look up to me now.' He turned to Ralph, but instead of saying 'hello' to his big friend, he pulled a face. 'Agh! Sticky webs! I forgot the ladybird juice.' And he ran back towards the house in a flap.

Ralph waited until Milton was out of leg-hair hearing. 'Aren't you sick of this, Audrey?'

'It's for a good cause,' she said, not sounding very convinced.

'I know, but . . . oh, ignore me. The sight of all this food I can't eat is making me grumpy. It's just . . . don't you miss the old days, before the *#NotScaredOfSpiders* campaign? Before Milton was famous and we could hang out and do proper spider things. Not fundraisers, or photo shoots, or sponsored woodlouse-eating competitions . . .

actually, that one I enjoyed. I'm fed up of serving vol-au-ants to snooty orb-weavers, and getting my claws glued together opening fan mail. All the "Oh, Milton, we love you so much, we want to have your spiderlings" is making his cephalothorax twice as big as it was before.'

'Hmm, he has changed,' agreed Audrey. 'Here, no one will miss a honey-roasted lacewing – eat it and cheer up. It's supposed to be a party.'

The fundraiser was a tremendous success, and attracted many species of local spider – jumping spiders, crab spiders, the event was glamorous enough even for a wasp spider to swing by, creating quite a stir. Food, ladybird juice and dark spaces were donated and their best garden spider friend, One Short, offered to build a new web for a group of homeless young orb-weavers every night for a week!

By the end of the evening everyone was exhausted.

'Let's clear up tomorrow,' said Audrey, pushing aside fruit-fly flan crumbs before sitting down beside Milton.

Milton leapt up. 'Too much to do. I still need to see Zoe and talk to her about the zoo promotion, and check the interweb for any messages from Hawaii. I've not heard from Dad in a while.' He bit his claw. 'And there's more fan mail to open . . .'

Ralph groaned.

'Surely it can wait until tomorrow?' Audrey asked gently.

'Well, not really. There'll be something else tomorrow. Come on, Audrey, you know better than that. Can you at least get those banners and bunting down?'

'Steady on, buddy,' said Ralph. 'Audrey's worked proper hard on this for you. Have you even said thanks?'

Audrey held her leg out to Ralph. 'It's fine, I don't mind. Milton's right, let's get this done, then we can relax tomorrow.'

'Well, you can, maybe,' said Milton, fussing over some spilt ladybird juice. 'I've got a photo shoot to organize with a company who are building a bridge almost as strong as a spider silk.' He rubbed his aching shoulders. 'Aha, there's Zoe now.' And with that, he sped off towards the house.

Being the approximate size of a raisin, 'sped' was a relative term, and by the time Milton reached the dining room, Zoe and her dad were halfway up the stairs.

He sighed and collapsed in a puffed-out heap on the table.

Typical.

What was less usual was that they were talking in a whisper and Mr Macey's arm was around Zoe as they walked. He gave her a re-assuring pat which piqued Milton's interest.

Something's wrong.

He strained his leg hairs to listen to the conversation as he dashed up the banister.

'. . . I'm sure he's fine, Zoe – you heard the

7

message, it was almost impossible to make out properly. Please try not to worry.'

'I hope he's OK. He's so tiny,' said Zoe, with a long sigh.

Milton hid in a gap.

What message? Is she worried about me? I am feeling pretty tiny right now.

Zoe glanced anxiously back down the stairs, past Milton, towards Mr M's phone which was still glowing on the table.

Milton took a deep breath and ran. He reached the phone just as the call list blinked off, back to black, but as he'd got closer Milton was sure he'd seen the word 'Hawaii' on the screen.

Fan Mail

'Are you all right, Milton?' said Audrey, hauling herself on to the table with her long legs. 'You look like you've seen the ghost of Old Hairy Lou.'

'I'm fine,' said Milton, jumping up and down on the phone.

'Let me try,' said Ralph. He climbed on to the edge of a half-drunk cup of tea and leapt on the phone screen. It came to life in a bright explosion of faces – Mr Macey's background was a hilarious picture of the three house humans with daft expressions. Zoe and Greta had glitter on their cheeks and Mr M was wearing red heart-shaped sunglasses.

It wasn't what Milton had seen a moment ago. 'Ralph, jump on it again. I'm sure I saw something about Hawaii on there.'

Ralph bounced up and down on the phone like a miniature hairy basketball. 'Mr M and Zoe would've told you if they had a message from your dad, surely?'

'Yes, of course. I'm just tired – I must be seeing things.' He smiled at Ralph, who was still pogoing on the screen. 'You can probably stop now.'

As they headed up to the attic, Milton thought of his dad.

He must've been on my mind for me to imagine seeing 'Hawaii' on the phone.

Before #NotScaredOfSpiders, Milton thought his dad was gone for ever. Then, thanks to the campaign, they'd reconnected using the human web. But somehow it made the distance between them feel even greater, and Milton wondered if he'd ever see his dad again.

*

Upstairs in their shared attic was a pile of Milton's fan mail under one of the eaves. Ralph yawned and stretched his hairy legs. 'Come on, then, Milt. Let's sort out this flippin' post of yours.' Since *#NotScaredOfSpiders* went global, Milton got a lot of mail, mostly drawings and letters from children who had been inspired to overcome their fears. Sometimes he received gifts – eight matching socks, abdomen polish, a tiny T-shirt with *#NotScaredOfHumans* on the front.

But he'd never had a parcel that moved before.

Ralph frowned, as the box, which was wrapped in brown paper and covered in tiny holes, jiggled across the attic floor.

'Do you think it's a bomb?' said Ralph, somewhat matter-of-factly.

'Don't bombs tick?' said Milton.

'Oh, yeah, that's right. What moves, then?'

'I don't know. It's making a scratching noise.'

'A jumping bean? Wind-up chattering teeth? A remote-control helicopter?'

'Perhaps you should open it.'

'Perhaps *you* should.' Ralph pushed the parcel over to Milton. 'It's yours after all.'

'You're in charge of deliveries.' Milton pushed the box back to Ralph, who sighed.

'It's just a box.' Ralph took a deep breath and looked inside. 'It's a cake,' he said. 'Look – from the Caterpillar Cupcake Company.' He brought out a little cupcake with pink frosting on top.

'Cakes don't move,' Milton said, scowling at the cake over the top of the box.

It shuddered for a moment, then suddenly a tiny speck of something leggy exploded out of the pink frosting. It did a mid-air somersault and landed in between Milton's front legs.

Milton screamed and fell over backwards. 'WHAT IS IT?' He squeezed his eyes shut and scrabbled to get upright and away until Ralph started laughing.

'Milt! Calm down.' Ralph plucked the tiny

creature from Milton's flailing claws and held it up. 'What have we here?' He wiped icing from its leg. 'Tasty.'

Milton opened his eyes and peered at the tiny creature.

'I'm a money spider,' grinned the little black dot in Ralph's legs. 'And I'm your number-one fan.' It waved a tiny flag at him, which Milton could just see had 'I ♥ Milton' drawn on in a spidery scrawl.

Milton let out a sigh, making the flag ripple. 'Great.'

He scowled. 'A fan. Just what I need.'

'This is so exciting. My name's Mini. You're my hero, I loved you on *Countryfile*.'

Ralph put the money spider down and pushed her over to Milton.

Milton did not look amused. 'Very clever. Now go home. I've got work to do.' It came out much harsher than Milton intended, but he was so tired and stressed and no one seemed to care.

Mini's almost microscopic fangs trembled and she sniffled.

'Milton!' exclaimed Ralph, looking uncharacteristically cross. 'You've upset her.'

Milton became agitated. 'What about how upset I am? I don't want followers, I don't want any of this.' He kicked aside the box that the money spider had delivered herself in and it knocked over the pile of unopened fan mail. 'Oh, sticky webs!' he shouted. 'I didn't organize the photo shoot!'

Milton suddenly came over very pale, ran

around in circles eight times, then slammed his front claws on the floor. 'I can't take it any more, Ralph. I'm a spider, not a celebrity. I've had enough. I just want to be left alone.'

And with that, he ran into the nearest dark hole and began to spin a web.

CHAPTER
3
Mini

Downstairs, Zoe was cleaning her teeth. She studied her expression in the mirror with curiosity, before rinsing. Something felt odd and it wasn't until her toothbrush rattled in the glass holder that she realized what it was.

The house was quiet.

Ever since they'd moved to the new house, the noise had changed. In the old days, Dad used to tuck Zoe in, then go back downstairs and watch a box set with the door shut, or read a book. Sometimes he listened to his favourite show tunes, but whichever it was, there was either silence, or a sort of low hum.

Now Greta was here, there was noise. There was laughing and chatting. And it was a cheerful sound, that filled the house with fun, and Dad was happy.

But for reasons Zoe couldn't figure out, it made her sad, and so it made no sense at all that tonight, with Greta away at a conference and with the old, familiar silence back, she felt even worse.

She got into bed. Probably she felt funny because of the phone message. Dad was right, it had been really hard to make out – she wasn't even sure it *was* about Milton's dad, maybe something about the mountain they were on in Hawaii? His human friend, Mako, sounded worried but perhaps it was nothing, just bad reception. Shaking off the feeling, she picked up her book, but had hardly read a page when Dad came in.

'So, how's things?' he said, leaning on the rail of her cabin bed.

Zoe put her book down. *Things* were, to be totally honest, weird. *Things* had been happening so quickly just lately, it was hard for her to keep up. First, they'd moved house and Greta had moved in with them, which was lovely and Dad was his old self again. But then there were SATs and the end of term coming and new school uniform to buy and the prospect of proper homework. And her current school friends had only just got their heads around her being a minor celebrity, so who only knew how people would feel about this at her new secondary school?

'Things are fine, Dad.' She held her dad's gaze. 'Honestly.'

Satisfied, her Dad stroked her hair and kissed her forehead. Zoe tried to let it soothe away all the worries she'd already thought of and the new one she'd added – that Milton's dad was possibly in trouble on a faraway volcano.

It was a big ask of one kiss.

Two days passed and Milton still had not emerged.

Audrey and Ralph had taken to sleeping on the floor outside the hole where Milton had webbed himself in, and they took turns to keep watch overnight.

They'd tried reasoning with him and bribing him. Ralph had tried to trick him out by pretending Steve Backshall was downstairs. Audrey had tried getting cross, and even Zoe had been up to the attic with the Nutella jar. But nothing worked. Milton had spun enough web to completely barricade himself in. The only way they even knew he was still there was because occasionally he would shout at them to go away and leave him alone.

'What are we going to do?' asked Ralph for the tenth time that evening.

'We could get One Short to have a go.' Audrey scratched her cephalothorax, otherwise out of ideas.

'She's building webs for the fundraiser raffle winners.' Ralph tickled Mini the money spider superfan under the abdomen and gave her a fly antenna to chew.

Audrey paced outside the hole. 'Milton? Are you at least eating in there?'

No answer.

'He can't be eating, Ralph. I'm so worried.'

'You hear that, buddy? Audrey's worried about you. She's looking very pale.'

'That won't work, Ralph. I always look pale.'

'We could chew our way in,' whispered Ralph.

'If this goes on much longer, we'll have to, otherwise he'll starve. But that's a last resort – he has to *want* to come out, or at least let one of us in.'

Just then, a tiny voice spoke up. 'I could help,' said the little speck on Ralph's back.

Ralph lowered Mini to the floor. 'Go on,' he said.

'I'm small enough to squeeze through even the tiniest gap. See there, at the entrance to the hole? It's a criss-cross of web, with teeny-weeny spaces. All it takes is someone small enough to fit through them.'

'You're a little genius!' Ralph clapped his front claws together. 'But once you're in there, how will you persuade him to come out?'

'Don't worry about that,' said Mini as she climbed on to the thick mat of web. 'I usually know what to say.'

Milton had done a thorough job of webbing himself off from the outside world, and as luck would have it, he'd found the perfect hiding hole. It was narrow at the entrance, gradually opening out into a round space. Most of the surround was brick, with a piece of felt flapping loose over a gap in the roof tiles.

What Audrey and Ralph didn't realize, from their vigil in the attic, was that from his refuge, Milton could climb on to the roof to catch bugs, or to get some fresh air, which was where he'd spent most of the last two days.

He sat, sheltered under a tile, staring up at the vast sky, watching the stars, and wondering if his dad was also gazing up at the moon, wherever he was.

Milton had always been prone to gloomy thoughts, but recently they seemed to have taken over. All he could think about was crawling into a dark hole and hiding from the world, the humans – even his friends.

I'm a rubbish spider. I'm a rubbish friend. I'm a false widow, but I feel like such a fake. Dad's

probably wondering why I haven't visited yet. Whatever must he think of me, playing at celebrity but then hiding in dark corners?

'I wanted to save my kind, but I can't even save myself,' he said to no one in particular.

And so he was rather surprised when a quiet voice answered from inside the hole, 'Of course you can't.'

'Who's there? How did you get in?' Milton climbed back inside and hugged his legs. 'What do you want?'

'I want to help you,' said Mini.

'No one can help me. Please leave me alone ... What do you mean, of course I can't save myself?'

'You're just one small spider. I know you saved your entire species and spoke to humans and started an internet campaign, but it doesn't change the fact: no one can do everything alone.'

Milton sighed. 'I'm sorry I was awful to you. I'm normally really nice.' He offered a leg to

Mini, but instead of shaking claws, Mini gave him a tiny hug.

'Don't worry about it. I understand. I know what it's like to be overwhelmed by the world. I'm so small, you'd imagine I'd never get anything useful done, but shall I tell you my secret?'

Milton nodded.

'I know when to ask for help.'

After a serious amount of jaw-aching chewing through web, Milton and Mini eventually emerged into the attic to face Audrey and Ralph. One Short had joined them after dawn, and they all stood in a row, anxiously twiddling claws and clicking their fangs.

'Sorry,' said Milton in a small voice.

Ralph bounded towards him and Milton breathed a sigh of relief. Ralph could always be relied on to forgive h—

But Ralph scooped up Mini instead and threw her into the air. As he caught her, he said,

'Mini! You little beauty, what did you do?'

Milton's legs wobbled.

'Everyone,' said Mini, 'Milton needs some space, and some quiet and a whole lot of help.'

Audrey looked at the floor. 'We have been helping, but it's getting too much.'

'Yeah,' said Ralph. 'We've replied to fan mail, hung bunting, made a gazillion ladybird cocktails.'

Mini crawled back to Milton and held his claw. 'Not that sort of help. Come and sit down and I'll explain.'

CHAPTER 4

Break Time

It was a warm Saturday morning, and Zoe and Greta were sitting on a rug in the garden, soaking up the sun, drinking fruit smoothies . . . and working. Both of them were surrounded by books and papers and wearing matching frowns.

Greta cracked her shoulder blades. 'Ugh, fancy having to work on a Saturday.' She looked sympathetically at Zoe.

'Tell me about it,' said Zoe, throwing a fluffy gel pen on to her notebook. 'What are you doing?'

'Trying to sort the paperwork for moving my

baby wolf spiders back to their natural habitat. It's not as easy as booking them on a flight. You can't transport animals to other countries without special permission. There are so many rules and regulations . . .' She drifted off, ticking another box on her form.

Zoe sighed and picked up her pen, wishing her friends weren't so far away now. The new house was great, with loads of space, but it was much further from school, and so far using this as a reason for Dad to give her a phone wasn't working.

Greta signed the document with a loopy scrawl and leant back, soaking up the sun. 'What are you working so hard on?'

Zoe frowned. Surely that was obvious? 'SATs next week,' she said.

'Oh my goodness!' Greta threw her arms up. 'I'm so sorry, of course it is. I've been so busy, how has it come around so soon? Can I help?'

'No, it's OK, Prof— I mean Gre— I mean . . . Mum.' Zoe winced.

'Oh, Zoe, you don't have to call me Mum, Greta's fine. Whatever you're comfortable with.' Zoe imagined her face made it clear that none of it was particularly comfortable. 'Dad would like it if I called you Mum.'

'I know, but I don't want you to think I'm trying to replace your mum, or be something I'm not. Maybe when we get married...'

Zoe looked at her spelling, punctuation and grammar, suddenly finding it fascinating. She had no idea what she wanted Greta to be, how she felt about them getting married, whenever *that* was happening, or where she, Zoe, even fit into her own family any more. Was she going to be like a spare wheel? The phrase 'two's company, three's a crowd' came to mind. Then Greta's phone rang, saving them both from the awkwardness of the conversation.

'It's your dad,' Greta said, unable to hide the relief in her voice.

Up in the attic the spiders sat in a semicircle,

with Mini in the middle.

'I'm a money spider. There are over four thousand types of money spider, and because we are so small, new species are being discovered all the time.'

Ralph tutted. 'Humans – terrible eyesight.'

Mini smiled. 'I'm a *Lepthyphantes tenuis*.' Mini made sure she said her scientific name slowly – *Lep-thee-fan-tees ten-you-is* – for the other spiders. 'We're the commonest spider in the UK. We're everywhere, so wherever I go, my family are not far away.'

Milton had a lump in his throat. 'My family is a long way from here. If he's even still alive.'

'Oh, Milton,' said Mini, rubbing his claw. 'Your family are right here with you now.'

Audrey took one long step forward. 'Mini's right. We're your family.'

Mini continued, 'Milton has been struggling with all the things going on in his head. He's had a lot to deal with. He's reconnected with his dad, he's become famous, humans are asking him to do new and strange things, and he feels responsible for other spiders because of the campaign. Those thoughts and ideas are like flies buzzing around in his head.' She turned to Milton. 'Your family can help you catch those thought-flies.'

'Yeah, we're here for you, buddy,' said Ralph. 'Tell us what you need.'

Milton closed his eyes. When Mini explained it like that, it all seemed so clear. 'I need a break,' he said.

As Milton was taking some time off in the attic, Zoe was downstairs, making a pile of baked beans on her plate.

'Eat up, sweetheart,' said Dad, eyeing her barely touched sausage and chips. 'You don't want your favourite dinner going cold.'

'I'm not that hungry,' said Zoe, as the bean heap collapsed.

'Well, try and eat something. You need to keep your strength up, keep those brain cells firing.'

Zoe looked blankly at her dinner and rubbed at the grey smudges under her eyes.

'How are the exams so far?' asked Dad.

Zoe sighed. 'OK, I guess. I think I'm doing all righ—'

She was cut off as Greta flew in through the door, dropping bags in the hall and flinging her coat on a chair. 'So sorry I'm late, guys.'

Dad got Greta's dinner out of the oven and popped it on the table as she swooped into her chair. 'Work is so busy,' she said, burning her mouth on a chip.

'Tell me about it,' said Dad. 'I've got so much on.'

Zoe sat quietly, eating tiny mouthfuls of sausage, watching Dad and Greta talking animatedly about their busy lives and wondered, if she got up from the table without making a sound, whether they'd even notice.

Then Greta turned to her. 'How's Milton today?'

Zoe grimaced. 'Oh, no! I haven't even

thought about him. He's out from hiding, but I forgot. I'm so awful. I'm an awful human.'

Then suddenly, she began to cry. Big whoopy gasps that she tried to cover up by shoving food in her mouth. It didn't work.

Dad and Greta both leapt from their seats and hugged her as she sobbed through a mouthful of chips.

'Oh, poppet. It's OK. What are we like? Going on about ourselves when you're so exhausted.' Dad stroked her hair. 'Milton will be fine. He's got his friends with him. Gosh, I guess everyone is feeling pretty stressed right now.'

Greta took her hand. 'One more day, then SATs will be over. Maybe we should do something special? Take a break – what do you think, Owen?'

'I think that's a great idea. We'll talk about it tonight. But for now, what would you like to do, Zoe? Shall we go and eat in front of the telly?'

'I'm really not hungry,' stuttered Zoe. 'But maybe . . . pudding?'

'Ice cream with sprinkles on?' Greta said. 'And *Dr Who*?'

'*Springwatch*?' suggested Dad.

Then they gave each other a knowing look and both said together, '*Moana*!'

Finally, Zoe's exams were done and the family had a tea party in the garden to celebrate. One half of the table was laid with sandwiches, fruit kebabs, party rings and crisps. The other half was a mouth-watering selection of ant bites, midge morsels, and dry-roasted millipede legs.

Mr Macey stayed well down his end of the buffet.

An air of relaxation settled over both humans and spiders, like a covering of blossom – all except for Mr Macey, who seemed distracted.

Milton didn't think it was just the fact that the centipede surprise was still wriggling.

'Mr M's acting weird,' he said to Audrey, who was stretched out under a cocktail umbrella. He turned to Mini. 'I've been studying human behaviour and I'm getting pretty good at it. For example, see Greta and Zoe there – Zoe has her arms crossed as Greta is pointing at her. It means Zoe wants to hug her. Very positive body language.'

Mini looked impressed.

'So trust me, Mr M is up to something.'

At that moment Mr Macey picked up a glass and tapped a spoon on the side. The tinkling sound brought everyone to attention.

'It's been a busy few weeks for us all, especially my darling Zoe. Whatever happens, you are smart and brilliant and we love you very much.'

Audrey put a claw to her abdomen. 'That's so lovely,' she said, wiping five of her eyes with a napkin.

Mr Macey's phone buzzed and he turned it face down. 'Here's to Zoe.' They raised their

glasses and everyone clapped.

'Greta has been working late and I've been pretty busy too. Basically, we're all in need of a holiday.'

Zoe gasped.

'So, without further ado – an announcement: this summer holiday, we're going to Hawaii!'

Zoe danced around the garden with Milton, jumping for joy, in her hand. She looked so happy it melted Milton's heart and he felt a sense of peace flow through him. This would be the break he needed and he would get to see his dad again. Everything was falling into place. It was all going to be OK.

That was why Mr M had been fidgety – he'd booked a surprise holiday. That was all it was. Wasn't it?

CHAPTER 5

Super-Suspicious Spider Smuggler

Three long months later, a very excited gang of humans and spiders arrived at departures in London Heathrow Airport's Terminal 3. As soon as they entered the enormous building, they all looked up. It was like being on a giant space station – silver beams and lights and people walking with purpose.

'This way,' said Zoe's dad, pointing at one of the many yellow signs suspended in the air.

Zoe had only been on an aeroplane once before, and was too young to remember. Her brain could barely keep up with all the information her eyes were sending it. Huge TV screens showed lists of flight numbers beside the names of exotic places she'd seen on maps, but had never properly felt were real. They'd seemed like fantasy worlds, but now here she was, at the portal to wondrous lands.

She secretly reached into her rucksack and pulled out a small, but very special box. It was hand-painted (by Zoe) and the lid had a swirl pattern of laser-cut holes. Zoe whispered into the holes, 'Guys, take a quick peek. This place is incredible!'

At once, twenty-four eyes appeared under the lid, although only twenty-one of them could see anything.

Milton waved one leg through a heart-shaped hole. This was the signal that they were fine. Two legs waving meant a problem. Like, for example, Dad or Greta discovering that Zoe had brought them along. They did not have passports after all. Or all those 'special permissions' that Greta had mentioned.

At first the airport was magical. It was

technically the start of the holiday, and Zoe imagined glamorous British Airways staff helping her with her bags, all smiles and treating her like an adult: *Zoe Macey, International Traveller*.

The magic wore off after the first twenty minutes of queuing.

Far from being glamorous, the airport was actually a series of waiting in line, yawning, fidgeting and shuffling, peppered with moments of extreme stress while finding passports and phones and looking as innocent as possible.

Security was the worst.

Because she was not Zoe Macey, International Traveller. She was Zoe Macey, Super-Suspicious Spider Smuggler.

The security queue was the longest. It snaked around in a huge, unfriendly and harshly bright space. Although, on this occasion, Zoe was grateful for the long wait – it gave her time to think.

Dad had explained that they needed to load

their bags in trays to go through an X-ray machine, then they'd walk through a scanning arch where they might need to take off their shoes, but she hadn't been able to picture it until now. The way he'd described it seemed easy, straightforward.

But it was not.

Tension hung in the air. Zoe picked up on the anxiety of the other travellers – what if we've accidentally packed scissors? Is there an oversized bottle of shampoo in my hand luggage? What if the dog put something in my pocket?

Do we take off our jewellery? Belts? Shoes? Watches? Hats? Nose piercings?

Ahhhhhhhhhhh!

Sweat began to bead around Zoe's forehead.

Dad and Greta were tussling over bags, trying to put the tablets and laptop in one tray and the money and keys in another, but the trays kept escaping along the conveyor belt. In the next queue along, a toddler was being told off for spinning around on his Trunki when it had to go through the X-ray. A security guard was arguing with a man whose bag was too big to go through the machine and they both tripped over a teenager who was sitting on the floor trying to untie her Doc Martens.

Zoe's heart beat faster and she looked at the special box in her bag.

'You can't go through the X-ray machine,' she whispered to it, keeping one eye on Dad and Greta, who were guzzling the last of their bottled water. 'They'll see you. You'll have to come through the arch with me.'

Two legs stuck up through the box holes and started waving.

'I know, but it's the only way through. Every-one and everything gets scanned. I can't wait for you to find a safe way through by yourselves – there are too many people and, anyway, this place is crazy! You'd get stepped on.'

Three pairs of legs now poked through the holes, waving frantically.

Zoe was unmoved. She pretended to drop her bag (carefully), and as she bent down to pick it up, she opened the box. 'Out. Now. Crawl up my sleeve and hide.'

The spiders exchanged extremely worried glances but did as they were told.

'It'll be fine,' said Zoe. 'This is the human world – you're going to have to trust me sometimes.' She giggled a little as they tickled her arm.

Zoe slung her bag into a tray, along with her hat and cardigan, and lined up to go through the arch.

Dad went through first and got the thumbs up from the security guard.

Then Greta. Also fine.

The guard motioned for Zoe to walk forward.

Taking a deep breath, she strode under the doorway-to-nowhere with as much confidence as she could muster, but as she passed through, the arch made a noise. Like that bleeping noise a computer makes when you've pressed the wrong key. Just an electronic sound, yet somehow it can make you feel like you've done something really, terribly wrong.

CHAPTER 6

Bradley O'Hair (Billionaire)

'Step over to me, love,' said the security guard. 'Shelly here will pat you down. Is this your mum and dad?' He pointed to Dad and Greta, and Zoe nodded, too terrified to speak.

'Routine one, folks. We check on a regular basis.'

Shelly stepped towards Zoe, wearing a pair of blue surgical gloves and holding a grey plastic paddle.

To Zoe's right, the man with the oversized bag was also being 'routinely checked'. He was very red in the face, and Zoe watched in horror as a guard swept his hands firmly along the man's arms, then patted down his sides.

Greta stepped forward. 'It's all right, Zoe, sweetheart. You haven't done anything wrong. They're just doing their job.'

Zoe tried to reply but her mouth was as dry as a camel spider's sand burrow.

'I promise I won't tickle too much.' Shelly smiled warmly.

Zoe tried to smile back and look normal and not like a spider-smuggling criminal who was about to get her friends squashed right in her elbow pit, when she burst out laughing.

'OK, then, Zoe, is it? Raise your arms like you're an aeroplane.'

Still giggling, Zoe did as she was told, but it was hard to stay still with three leggy spiders scuttling up her arm. She fought the urge to slam her arms down as they reached her armpit, and instead she puffed out her cheeks and went as red as Mr Huge Bag. As Shelly swept her legs, Zoe wriggled and arched as the spiders crossed her shoulder blades, then she had to fake a sneeze as they wriggled out of her T-shirt and into her hair.

'My, you *are* a ticklish one,' said Shelly as she stood up. 'OK, you're all done. Have a great holiday.'

Zoe leant forward with her hands on her knees, and breathed out, as Dad and Greta began the frantic exercise of putting everything back in the bags. As they reattached brooches and belts and debated which pocket the passports were supposed to go in, Zoe grabbed her bag.

'Well done, guys. That was a close one,' she said, helping Milton, Audrey and Ralph back into the box. Then she gave her head a good scratch. 'Well, this holiday can't get any worse than that.'

Getting on the plane was like entering a new world. Zoe was allowed the window seat, and she got to watch an in-flight movie (while the spiders argued over whose turn it was to watch through the box lid). Then she had a snooze while listening to music on the plane radio until human food arrived in a little tray.

In the box, the spiders tucked into their travel snacks and chattered excitedly about the holiday.

They were actually flying to Hawaii!

And then it hit Milton. He was flying to find his dad.

His stomach churned in his cephalothorax and he gripped the side of the box.

What is wrong with me?

'You OK, Milt?' asked Ralph.

'Sure, don't think I'm a natural flyer is all.'

'It doesn't feel like when I flew. But then I was tied to a toy soldier. Good job he knew what to do with that parachute, I was terrified!'

Milton gave a small smile but he wasn't feeling right at all. He was weirdly worried about seeing his dad.

'Get some rest, Milton. You'll be fine.'

My inner voice is sounding squeaky. And

rather optimistic. Perhaps I'm coming down with something.

'Mini?' cried Audrey and Ralph.

'Hello!' Mini grinned as though suddenly appearing nine thousand metres above the Atlantic Ocean was the most normal thing in the world.

'What are you doing here?' said Ralph, giving her the most delicate squeeze he could.

She pointed to her tiny T-shirt, which Ralph had to squint with all his eyes to see. It had 'I ♥ Milton' on the front. 'I'm his number-one fan, remember?'

'Sure, but . . . how did you get here?' said Audrey. 'We had a nightmare getting through security.'

'Oh, you know me, I'm so small that literally no one notices.'

'You're a stowaway on top of stowaways?' Milton gasped. 'But I'm glad you're here. Come on, you can sleep by me. It sounds like you've had a busy day.'

*

It was a long flight, with a stopover in Los Angeles, USA, which meant they had to get off the big plane, wait in a different airport (that weirdly looked exactly like the last one) and get on another smaller plane before they finally reached Hilo International Airport.

The excitement of travelling had definitely worn off and everyone was tired and grumbling about the weight of the suitcases and where they would get a taxi.

'Doesn't someone wait at the exit holding a sign with our names on?' said Zoe wearily.

Greta and Dad scanned the airport signs. 'I think that's only for tour buses and celebrities,' Dad said distractedly. Zoe checked out all the signs anyway.

The Porters
Mr Horvath
Kau Wela Vacations
The Maceys

'Dad!' Zoe grabbed her dad's sleeve. 'We've

49

got one! Are we famous here too? We *are* celebrities!'

Dad looked at Greta as if she might know what was going on, but she shook her head. 'Maybe there are other Maceys?'

The man with the sign waved his mobile phone at them. 'Hey there, you Owen and Greta Macey?'

That was the second time someone had mistaken Greta for her mum, but Zoe decided to ignore it. He *was* there for them! She leapt with delight, suddenly wide awake again. Then she remembered her precious cargo. 'Sorry,' she muttered to her bag.

As the man approached he finished his call, wincing as he hit 'speaker' instead of the hang-up button and a loud, mechanical sawing noise screamed from the phone. 'Sorry about that,' he said as Dad walked over to him.

'Hi, yes, I'm Owen Macey.' He looked confused. 'Did someone send you?'

'Sure did, buddy. Me! The name's Bradley O'Hair. Owner of the Big Bradley Beach Hotel. Pleasure to meet you, folks.' He held out his hand and Zoe's dad shook it.

'Owen Macey. And this is Greta, my fiancée and Zoe, my daughter.'

'This is the world-famous Zoe Macey, who likes spiders so much.'

Zoe was sure Bradley sneered as he spoke,

but then he gave a little bow and his baseball cap fell off and she figured she was mistaken. 'Nice to meet you, Mr O'Hair. Have you got a limousine?'

'Zoe!' scolded Dad. Then, 'Have you?'

'Sorry, friends, the limo is being restocked today – topping up the curly straws and cocktail umbrella supplies. I do love a little umbrella in my drink, don't you?' He didn't wait for an answer. 'I'm sure you'll be very comfortable in my little car.'

Zoe handed Bradley his cap back, raising a swift eyebrow at the picture of Bradley's face on the front, surrounded by colourful hibiscus flowers and hearts. Across the middle of the logo were the words: *BOB – Bradley O'Hair (Billionaire)*.

The 'little car' was an enormous four-by-four, bright red with BOB logos on all the doors and the bonnet. Bradley's driver took their luggage and they all piled into the vehicle. Bradley got in last, grinning broadly at them all.

Zoe could barely take her eyes off the man – he looked like a cartoon character, with a permanent smile, and he was wearing the most alarming colour combinations. His shorts were salmon-pink and his blindingly bright Hawaiian shirt was purple, orange and green. Teamed with the red cap, it threatened to give Zoe a headache. And it all looked very out of place with his mud-caked work boots.

'I can't tell you how thrilled we are to have you here, you guys. When my assistant mentioned your name had come up in the bookings I just knew I had to meet y'all.' He handed them some tickets from his pocket. 'Complimentary passes for the cinema I own in town, and free coffees, and surfing lessons. Your family are going to have the best time at my place. You won't need to go anywhere else. We have the best spa facilities in the US, best pools, best cocktails, best beds – the comfiest beds you'll ever find. That flight from England is a long one, for sure – and, well, we are going to look after you and then some. Mr Macey, you play golf?'

'Er, no. Sorry.'

Bradley's face fell. Zoe thought for a millisecond that he might cry, or hit an ejector button and fling them all into the sea. But he fixed his smile back on and said, 'I'm sure that's because you've not been to the best golf course yet. I'm gonna take you golfing just as soon as you've unpacked.' He slapped Mr Macey on the back, and Zoe smirked as her dad's mouth gave a little twitch of horror.

Bradley talked pretty much all the way to the hotel. Mostly about his businesses – it turned out he owned a lot of things on the island and they were all the best. Best surfing, best coffee, best real estate (which Dad explained meant 'best houses') and, as they pulled into the hotel car park, she realized that what Bradley might actually be best at was exaggerating.

CHAPTER 7

Everything Is Awesome

It would take a while to get used to the new time zone, the heat and the hotel itself, which Mr M had taken to describing as 'full of character'.

Ralph eventually got his cephalothorax around the fact that although they were supposed to be lying low, it was fine for them to sunbathe on the fifth-floor window ledge. Zoe had even made them a tiny pool out of a soap dish, so they could have a proper holiday experience.

'The only thing missing is room service,' said Ralph, groaning as he got to his claws to grab a beetle from the snack box.

'This is certainly the life,' said Milton. 'I've not thought about promotions, publicity or portrait photos for ages.' He paused. 'Well, except just then. I wonder what's happening to all the fan mail.'

Audrey propped herself up on her long front legs. 'Don't you dare.'

'I'm just thinking of all the fans who won't be

getting replies, and how it'll all be waiting for me when I get back . . .' He stopped. Audrey was giving him that look again. 'We're on holiday. You need to relax, remember? That was the whole point of coming here.'

'And to see Dad,' said Milton. A shadow fell across his face, but it was just a butterfly.

'What's the plan there, then? Web-swing to the forest, find the old fella, then back in time for a damselfly dinner?' Ralph rubbed his front claws together in anticipation.

Audrey looked out of the window to the horizon. 'It's an awfully long way. I can only just see the edge of the rainforest from here.'

Milton nodded in vigorous agreement. 'Waaay too far. I've not been keeping up my web-swinging either. And you wouldn't be able to come, Ralph.'

'Don't use me as an excuse – I can zip wire on your web.'

'Swing on someone else's web? That sounds very wrong. You're not swinging on mine.'

Milton grimaced. 'I don't think we should rush into things until we know exactly where Dad is. I was chatting to Zoe yesterday and she thinks Greta and Mr M are up to something. That there's more to this holiday than meets her two eyes. Like a surprise about my dad?'

'Milton, your dad is an international explorer – he's fine. Stop trying to find things to worry about.' Audrey's expression was bordering on cross.

'Well Zoe is going to keep her ear to the ground.'

'That'll make walking tricky for her. That Zoe, she'd do anything for you, Milt.' Ralph stretched out on the ledge again, looking down at the humans below. 'Funny place, this. Look at them all, lying there like larvae.'

Ralph was fascinated by the hotel, and Milton had to explain to him on more than one occasion that they didn't live here now, they were just borrowing the room and that Bradley owned the whole place. Milton was only beginning to understand money, but he was sure there must be something better to do with it than buy a great big house and put your face all over the soft furnishings. Then Zoe had started unpacking her things, arranging her tablet, books and her beloved fluffy tarantula on the desk, explaining that she was 'making herself at home'. At this point Ralph had given up trying to make sense of it and got on with finding the best corner for eating, sleeping and taking it easy in general. Which, for Ralph, was pretty much anywhere.

'Anyone for a bit of para-leaf-gliding later this afternoon?' Milton said, feeling the direction of the wind with his claw.

'I will,' said a voice from out of nowhere.

Ralph clutched his abdomen. 'Honestly, Mini, you're going to give me a heart attack one of these days. Where did you appear from this time?'

'I just floated in on the breeze,' she said cheerfully. 'I'm glad you're starting to relax,

Milton. This is a holiday, remember? No drama, no danger, just a lovely family reunion.'

The next morning at breakfast, silence weighed heavily at the Maceys' table. No one spoke. An occasional look was exchanged, but otherwise nothing.

Except chewing.

Eventually, Zoe's dad broke the spell. 'You two are absolute animals!'

Zoe and Greta responded by nodding enthusiastically and making disgusting grunting noises, their mouths stuffed full of the local cuisine. 'I mean, what even is that, Zoe?'

'It's *loco moco*,' she replied, in a tone that said, *Duh, you heard me order it.*

'Right . . . but what is it?'

Zoe pointed to the collapsing mountain of food. 'Egg, burger, rice, gravy.' Then shovelled in some more. 'It's del-ish-us.' A bit of rice flew on to the table.

Dad looked at his toast and jam for comfort.

'I'm having that tomorrow,' said Greta. 'It looks amazing – Hawaiian food is the best! Do you want to try my bacon and pineapple bake?' She offered a forkful of what looked like pizza topping to Dad, who hid behind his BOB-branded coffee cup.

'I'll pass, I think, sweetheart.'

'Well, at least the food is good.' Greta gazed around the dining room. 'It's not *quite* what I was expecting.'

Owen sniggered. The hotel was certainly different – seemingly decorated to match Bradley's fashion sense. There was more colour on the wall than a DIY store after an explosion, and almost everything that could be was made of pink plastic – the cutlery, the chairs and the staff's shoes. The option to Go Large was available on everything, and on the walls were photos and blueprints of what Bradley had described as his 'moments of entrepreneurial genius'.

There was a drawing of a petrol-powered

wave machine to improve the surf, a plan for drilling into the volcano to fuel lava-powered barbeques and, most ridiculous of all, a giant magnet to attract all of Bradley's lost golf balls – he'd had them custom-made with metal centres, and it was a miracle only a flock of nene geese got hit.

But whatever the surroundings, it was a fun family breakfast. Everything was calm. Everyone was happy. No one was fretting about work, or exams, or whatever else Dad and Greta had going on. Life was good.

Which is why, of course, everything was about to go wrong.

'What's the plan for finding Milton's dad, then?' asked Zoe as she finished off a second peanut butter smoothie. 'Is he in trouble?' She made an unnecessarily loud noise as she hoovered up milk and ice cream with her straw. 'And if so, how do we find a tiny false widow in a vast leafy rainforest?'

Owen squirmed, *umm*ing and *ahh*ing, but was saved from not having a good answer by one of the waiting staff.

'Mr Macey? Someone just left this at the desk for you.' Zoe's dad took the piece of folded paper, read it, looked shifty, then pushed out his chair and stood up.

And sat back down immediately, a startled expression on his face.

The pink chandelier tinkled above them, shaking gently at first, then violently. Zoe and Greta got up too, and realized why Owen had taken his seat again so suddenly. The floor was moving.

Cutlery rattled, the ketchup bottles fell over and an elaborately framed picture of a boy with scruffy hair crashed to the floor.

Bradley himself staggered into the room. 'It's all fine, folks,' he said, making calming gestures with his hands. 'Just a small one. The hotel is built for this kinda thing.'

'Is it an earthquake?' asked Greta.

'Yup, because of the volcano. We get 'em every now and again. Nothing to worry about.' He grinned, showing all his teeth, which he seemed to think was reassuring. And then the shaking stopped. 'There we go, everyone, drinks on the house. No problem, it's all good.'

'That's very kind, Mr O'Hair,' said Owen, getting up again. 'Especially on top of all the free vouchers you've given us. It's almost as if you want us to enjoy ourselves here!'

'You Brits, so funny.' Bradley shook Owen's hand vigorously.

'Is the volcano going to erupt?' asked Zoe, a little too loudly.

Bradley's face went from sunset orange to faded peach. 'Not at all, this happens all the time. All the time. Anyway, I'd like to offer your parents an afternoon in our spa. On the house. The whole afternoon, then dinner in the restaurant.'

Zoe opened her mouth to inform Bradley once and for all that Greta was not her parent, but she couldn't get a word in edgeways.

'We were going out to eat tonight,' said Greta.

'No need,' said Bradley. 'The best food on the island is right here, you don't have to set foot outside the hotel. This one agrees, am I right?' He pointed at Zoe's plate, which she had practically licked clean.

'Well, the spa does sound nice. We did come here to relax. We can do the *other* stuff tomorrow.' That look again between Greta and Dad – the one that was only for them.

'And for the little one, free movies on the Billionaire Channel all week. Especially for you.'

Little one.

Before Zoe could argue the point about being eleven, and nearly twelve, actually, Bradley gave them a cheesy grin, two thumbs up, and galumphed over to the next table, retrieving the fallen photo as he went.

Owen had another, more successful go at standing. 'Just popping out for a sec.' And he walked into the foyer.

Zoe and Greta eyed the note he'd left behind on the table. They both made a grab for it, but Zoe was faster.

Red Badger, Island Fox is outside

O...K...

Greta conveniently had to use the loo all of a sudden, leaving Zoe to consider this highly suspicious turn of events.

She leant back on her chair as far as she dared without tipping over and could just make out her dad in the foyer. He seemed to be whispering to a bearded Hawaiian man hiding behind a fake palm tree. This was too interesting to miss. Zoe casually strolled to the cutlery bench in order to get a better look. As she pretended to rate the teaspoons, she saw a teenage girl join Palm-Tree Man and her dad. The girl had long dark hair, plaited down the back, a short khaki skirt and seriously cool high-tops. Her hands were glued to her hips and even at a distance Zoe could see she was directing an impressive eyebrow raise towards the foliage.

Just then, two of the staff came running over to the palm tree. There was a lot of shaking of plastic leaves, then the man and the teenage girl were escorted roughly out of Zoe's view and presumably out of the hotel. The staff were frowning as they spoke to Dad, then Greta appeared and led him away and back to their table.

'Ah, the perfect teaspoon,' said Zoe smiling innocently as they walked past, although once back at the table, she couldn't hide the fact that she didn't even need a spoon.

'What was that all about, Red Badger?' Zoe passed him the note as Greta sat down again too.

Owen made a caught-singing-into-a-hairbrush expression and stuffed the note in his pocket. 'Ah. I have a confession. Before you hit the gold-and-purple-carpeted ceiling, I want you to know that we *are* on holiday. But Greta and I have been trying to kill two birds with one stone, make hay while the sun shines, and all that . . . ' Owen looked as if he'd lost his own thread.

'What are you on about?' said Zoe, managing to shove her hands on her hips, even sitting down.

Greta interrupted. 'Island Fox is Mako Gonzalez, the wildlife photographer and journalist Milton's dad has been travelling with. Being somewhat dramatic, I might add.' She turned to Owen. 'Is everything OK?'

'No . . . it's worse than we thought – Mako has heard rumours that someone is bulldozing part of the rainforest up on the mountain. He doesn't know for sure who, but he has his suspicions.'

Zoe remembered Bradley's noisy phone call at the airport and the mud on his boots. She picked up a BOB takeaway cup and crushed it, twisting Bradley's face into a snarl. 'It must be him!'

'Let's not jump to any conclusions. We're guests in his hotel, so we need to be careful.' Greta popped the cup back on the table.

'Mako and his daughter, Jenna, have already got themselves banned from all of Bradley's businesses on the island. They've been branded "troublemakers".'

Zoe nodded. They were now the ones on the inside. A plan began to form in Zoe's head, including putting those awesome trainers Jenna was wearing on her Christmas list. 'That's not all,' said Owen. 'Mako said there was a thriving colony of Hawaiian happy-face spiders in that area of the forest. If the trees are cut down they'll be wiped out . . . and Milton's dad is with them.'

CHAPTER
9
Private (Eight) Eyes

Zoe burst into her room. 'Guys! Milton – I need to talk to you about your dad.' She checked the window ledge and their newly constructed 'cobweb corner', but the spiders weren't there. 'Guys?'

Zoe squinted at the dark places in the room. 'Milton? Audrey? Ralph? Where are you?' She lifted the lid of the little wooden box and found the three arachnids curled up in a ball, their abdomens rising and falling rhythmically.

'Good morning!' She tickled Ralph, not even noticing Mini, who was snuggled under one of Ralph's hairy legs like a cuddly toy. In her defence, Ralph did sometimes take snacks to bed.

'Bluebottle pie!' Ralph shouted, waking up with a start. He stretched and shook the others, who yawned and crawled sluggishly on to Zoe's hand. She took them to the Spida-Com, almost dropping them on to it in her excitement.

'Wake up. Something's happened. And I don't just mean the earthquake you all slept through.'

Ralph rubbed his eyes. 'I hope it's lunch.'

Audrey stretched out her long legs one at a time then tapped the Scrabble tiles:

WHERE WERE YOU

Milton joined her.

WE GOT BORED BY THE POOL

Then Ralph tapped:

AND HUNGRY

THIS HOTEL IS TOO CLEAN

Ralph's tummy growled to make his point.

'I'm sorry,' said Zoe. ' You eat a lot more bugs than I realized. Our house must be teeming with them. I'll find you something to eat in a minute. But listen, something just happened at breakfast.'

Zoe told them all about Red Badger and Island Fox (which was somewhat confusing for the spiders at first).

'So, to cut a long story short . . .' She shot a quick glance at Ralph whose long stories were legendary. 'Milton, your dad has been living with a group of Hawaiian happy-face spiders on the slopes of an active volcano, and is surrounded by diggers and bulldozers, in terrible danger. His house human, Mako, has asked my Dad and Greta to help.'

Milton paled, staggered backwards into Audrey and seemed to just catch himself short of fainting.

Perhaps the longer version might have been a bit more subtle.

Ralph tapped, looking proud of how his spelling was improving.

'We're going to have to rescue him,' said Zoe.

Two hours later, in the small hotel library, the spiders were clutching their abdomens and groaning, having stuffed themselves with their own local breakfast (or, more accurately, brunch, as it was now – well, who knew what time it was?)

Zoe had squeezed in one more peanut butter smoothie and was just putting the finishing touches to the first Private (Eight) Eye Investigations case file.

It was a little thin on notes, but the cover was pretty.

Zoe pushed her dark glasses down over her nose. She was wearing them indoors so as not to draw attention to herself, but it was actually quite hard to see.

'Feeling better?' she asked the spiders.

They looked at her, fit to burst, and nodded. The library was very dusty, full of old cobwebs and flies – unlike anywhere else in the spotless hotel. When Zoe had requested her drink be brought there, the staff had to have a discussion to determine exactly where the library was.

'We have a library? That's news to me,' the bartender had said. Zoe asked the cleaning staff, but they had never heard of it either.

It was perfect for a secret meeting with three peckish spiders.

'So, before we go heading off into danger, we need proof that Bradley O'Hair, the so-called billionaire, is behind the destruction of the happy-faces' habitat. This is what I have so far,' said Zoe, tapping the case file with her green gel pen. 'Milton's dad is trapped on Mount Kilauea. Which is a volcano. Potential issue, given the minor earthquake this morning, but moving on. Someone is bulldozing the mountain – why? It sounds like a hair-brained scheme to me. And who is the king of O'Hair-brained schemes around here?'

Ralph shrugged, so Audrey and Milton nudged him from either side, squeezing out a little fruit-fly flavoured burp.

'Oh, right,' he said. 'O'Hair. I get it.'

Zoe continued. 'You guys probably haven't seen the picture of the pink polystyrene beach that blew away, have you? The man is an environmental disaster – he's our prime suspect, but we need more evidence before we can do anything. So far all we have is a load of golf courses, hotels, limos, jet skis, yachts and possibly one private jet, but we need something to link him specifically to the deforestation on Kilauea.'

Audrey lowered herself from a shelved copy of *The 50 Biggest Hotels in the World* on a long thread of silk, then swung herself back and forth until she had enough speed to knock into a row of takeaway cups that were lined up like dominoes.

'Yes, Audrey. All the single-use plastic is terrible, but we need something that places him directly at the scene of the crime.' Zoe tapped her chin with the pen. 'Mako and his daughter, Jenna, are already banned from the hotel and the staff saw them talking to Dad and looked pretty cross. They could be on to us already. We'll have to be very careful. This is turning into an extremely dangerous mission.' She watched

Audrey climb back up the bookcase like a graceful mountaineer. 'That's it, Audrey. We're going to have to climb the mountain and see for ourselves!'

Audrey slipped back down two shelves in shock.

She spun round and gave Zoe one of her fiercest looks, which even Zoe was getting to be scared of.

'Where else will we get the proof we need and rescue Milton's dad? Unless anyone's got a better idea?' Zoe slumped back into the enormous old leather armchair and looked thoughtful.

After almost a minute's silence, Ralph raised his leg.

CHAPTER 10

The Man with the Golden Toilet

As per Ralph's daring plan, Zoe left Milton, Audrey and Ralph in another, smaller plastic pot plant on the tenth floor of the hotel, and went off to lunch by the pool, with Greta and her dad.

Operation Spy-der was GO!

All the spiders had to do was sneak into Bradley's office.

Milton and Audrey slipped through the keyhole and spun a thread to the garishly carpeted floor.

But Ralph was stuck.

'How do you get up the plughole and you

can't fit through there?' said Milton.

'You, for one, should know that's a common misconception. I don't go up the plughole. I fall down into the bath.'

'I'll get him,' said Audrey, and climbed, leg over leg, back up to the gold door handle.

'Maybe you shouldn't have had that last ambrosia beetle,' she said, shaking her head.

'They were so tasty. And tiny, really.' Ralph hung his cephalothorax, which was safely in the office. His abdomen was firmly stuck back in the hallway. 'This is possibly the most embarrassing thing that's ever happened to me,' he said, wriggling.

Audrey hoisted up her silk thread. 'I very much doubt that. Here, tuck your legs in.' She looped the thread up and over him and tied it underneath. 'Think thin thoughts.'

'That's easy for you to say,' said Ralph, but too late – Audrey jumped.

'Ooooooooowwwwwwwww!' Ralph pop-ped out of the keyhole like a cork from a bottle

and flew all the way to Bradley O'Hair's desk, where he landed on an open laptop. With Audrey still attached, he began sliding backwards, and the movement brought the laptop screen to life.

'Guys, come up here. I've found something,' he called.

Milton and Audrey clambered up, Audrey rubbing her head where she'd hit it on the table leg.

'It's a video,' said Milton. 'Of the rainforest. And look, there's the BOB logo.'

'If it's a video, why isn't it moving?' asked Ralph.

'We need to activate that triangle on the screen. Wriggle around on that square bit, like you do with Zoe's laptop and see what happens.'

Ralph shimmied down and as he wiped his bottom on the mouse pad, an arrow shape appeared.

'That's it.' Audrey clapped her front claws together. 'Now move the arrow pointer to the triangle.'

Ralph shook his head. 'Squares, arrowy pointy triangles? How is this my life?' But he did it. The pointer rested on the play button. 'Now what?'

The spiders exchanged looks.

'Click it,' said Milton.

'Right,' said Ralph. 'Um . . .' He crossed his claws together and clicked. 'Did that help?'

'No! We need to click the button. The play button. The triangle!'

'Oh, for goodness' sake, I don't know!' Ralph sat down hard on the mouse pad, which depressed underneath him.

And clicked.

Suddenly an almighty noise came from the laptop, as on the video, diggers and chainsaws sprang into life. Milton, Audrey and Ralph fell backwards in alarm as they watched humans in flowery hi-vis jackets cutting down trees and bulldozing the ground. The camera panned round to take in the extent of the destruction – shrubs uprooted, the broken limbs of trees lay all around, and the ground was churned like a farmer's field. The spiders had just got to their claws again when, on-screen, Bradley suddenly leapt into view, photobombing his own video. This caused great confusion and alarm when the real Bradley O'Hair burst through the office door, roaring into his mobile phone.

The spiders screamed and grabbed one another.

'Chuck, you're a great guy,' he boomed into the phone, 'but I gotta go, I think these eco-crazy Maceys are on to me – I just caught them with that journalist. Sure, it's under control – I'm just going to stop them going up there, with free stuff and golf. That usually works. I ain't letting a few stupid trees stand in my way, or even fewer stupid tree huggers. I'm Bradley O'Haaaaaaaaaaaaaaay!' Bradley threw his phone into the air as he saw the spiders clutching on to one another on his keyboard.

'Eeeeeeewwwwwww – disgusting!' he squeal-ed in a high-pitched voice, grabbing a slipper with his face on. He whipped it behind him to splat the spiders, then stopped and made a gagging sound. 'I can't even squash you – I'll have spider parts in my laptop.' He tipped his head. 'What the heck, I'll buy another laptop.'

Bradley picked up the computer by the very corner of the screen and walked it over to the window. He was about to throw it out, spiders and all, until he seemed to realize that probably wouldn't go down well with the guests sunbathing thirty metres below. So he turned and ran to the bathroom. Milton thought he was scared before, but the thought of falling from a great height into someone's belly button was nothing compared to the shock of being in the billionaire's bathroom. It was all gold and mirrors and Milton couldn't work out what was real and what was a reflection and then he realized they were hanging over the toilet. Bradley started to shake the laptop violently, and Milton slipped from the Y key all the way to the Q.

Audrey gasped and grabbed him with her long legs at full reach, all the while spinning frantically to secure them to the USB drive that was sticking out of the side of the laptop.

'I don't want to die on holiday,' wailed Ralph.

'And, I refuse to be flushed down the loo. Even if it is gold-plated.' Audrey had a fierce look on her face as she tied her silk thread tightly around Milton, then Ralph. 'Hold on to me,' she said.

Being so slender and delicate, there wasn't much to hang on to, but Milton and Ralph put a leg around her and grabbed one another. Ralph gave Audrey a small kiss on the cheek.

'What was that for?' She blushed.

'For luck. Saw it on the telly.' He gave Audrey a wonky smile, then she took a deep breath and leapt into the air.

Ralph and Milton were a little heavier than she'd anticipated and instead of performing a long, loopy swing they plummeted towards the toilet bowl.

AHHHHHHHHHHHHHHHHHHHHHH!

Bradley saw the dangling bundle of spiders and screwed up his face like a giant baby about to let out a huge, red-faced cry. He flung the laptop into the air, just as the spiders were about to disappear past the golden seat. The web rope snapped back like a bungee, flinging the spiders up, then all too quickly they were falling again. The ball of Milton, Ralph and Audrey hit the gold-flecked marble sink, bounced off and landed squarely in the bin.

'Oh, my head,' said Milton, crawling to get on top of the pile of screwed-up paper they had landed in.

Audrey pushed Ralph off her. 'Oh, *your* head,' she said. 'It's squashing me.'

'Sorry, Audrey,' groaned Ralph, wriggling off her tiny body. 'Are you all right? You saved us, you know.'

'I'm not sure I did,' she said and started to bury herself under the paper. Milton looked up to see Bradley staring down at them.

'Gross,' he said. 'You're as bad as those horrid happy-face things. Well, you won't beat me in the War On Bugs. This hotel is losing enough money as it is, without the scandal of an insect infestation.' And before the spiders could protest about being arachnids, not insects, he sprayed them square in the face with the nearest thing to hand: a huge crystal-cut bottle of *Man des Toilettes*, then ran out, slamming the door behind him.

CHAPTER 11
Discovery!

The spiders had no idea how long they were unconscious.

Fortunately Bradley's aftershave, although utterly revolting, was harmless, and all they were left with was a fog of cloying perfume and a slight headache.

Milton was the last to come round and was groggy and miserable as he rubbed his eyes. 'So much for getting away from the stresses of my life. I'm sitting in rubbish!' He collapsed against a can of hairspray. 'We're never going to be able to help Dad.'

Audrey wiped her good eyes with a receipt.

'*That* was disgusting. Bradley is an awful human. Don't you worry, Milton. We'll stop him.'

'Audrey's right,' agreed Ralph. 'Also, if you don't mind me saying, you seem a bit more like your old self, Milt.'

Milton sniffed his claws and grimaced. 'Really?'

'Yeah. I could be wrong but I don't think the celebrity life suits you. You're your dad's son, an adventurer at heart.'

Milton wished for eyebrows to raise, Zoe did that so effectively in situations like this.

Audrey nodded at Ralph's unexpected wisdom. 'Ralph's right, Milton. I know you're worried for your dad, but admit it, you're enjoying all this investigating, problem-solving—'

'Sticking your kephalo-doo-dah in other people's business,' interrupted Ralph.

Milton wasn't so sure. He *was* feeling better since his 'incident' in the attic, but surely this was worse – coughing up aroma of O'Hair in a bin?

'I don't know, I never got almost flushed down the loo on photo shoots.'

'You're a thrill seeker, mate. Accept it.' Ralph looked pleased with himself.

Eager to change the subject, Milton said, 'We're no closer to getting any evidence for Zoe. That awful video is on Bradley's laptop, which looks broken, not that we could get it to her anyway. We need something she can stick in the book.'

Ralph was heading to the rim of the bin when he stopped and looked down at the crumpled piece of BOB headed paper beneath his claws. 'Guys, come and look at this. It might be what we've been looking for. Maybe. My reading's getting better, but, crikey, his hand-writing is bad.'

'It's a to-do list,' said Audrey, running her front leg over the words. 'Zoe writes them all the time. It's a list of stuff you need to get done, but have no intention of actually doing.'

'OK, let's assume it's Bradley's, since it's in his

bathroom. What's on the list?'

Audrey carried on reading aloud:

- play golf ✓
- go jet-skiing ✓
- have hair done ✓
- play golf ✓
- get nails buffed ✓
- invent new fruit cocktail and name it after me ✓
- bulldoze the forest to build a golf course ✓
- play golf ✓
- pluck eyebrows ✓

Milton gasped. 'All Bradley's to-do items are ticked. Maybe Bradley actually does the stuff on his lists. Ralph, you're a genius. This is the proof we need that Bradley is behind the destruction.'

'But how do we get this to Zoe? It's too big to bring with us . . . isn't it?' Ralph side-eyed Audrey, as though he knew what she was going to say.

'We only need that one item from the list.

We can nibble that out and Ralph can carry it. What do you think, Ralph? You're so strong and capable.'

Ralph couldn't refuse Audrey when she called him strong. He didn't know what capable meant, so he let that one go, but it sounded good. 'Fine. Let's get on with it before Bradley O'Must Get My Hair Done Again comes back.' He exercised his jaw in preparation. 'Ugh, I hate chewing up bits of paper.'

Zoe and Greta were sharing a plate of *laulau*, *lomi-lomi* salmon and *poi*, while Dad looked at them nervously and ate a cheese and ham toastie. He wrinkled his nose. 'What *is* that stuff you two are eating? It looks like a purple jellyfish.'

'Oh, Dad, you're so unadventurous. Have you heard from Mako yet? What's the plan to expose Mr O'Hair as a tree-killer?'

Greta dipped a piece of fish in the *poi* and shushed Zoe.

'Oh, come on – plastic straws? Polystyrene cups? And no one walks anywhere in this hotel. Have you seen all the golf buggies? It's got to be him, remember he had mud on his boots when we arrived? I bet he'd come straight from digging up the mountain.'

Dad sighed. 'Mud isn't proof, Zoe. But we should go and take a look,' he said. 'There's a great visitor centre in the national park. We can't come all this way without seeing a volcano, right? We'll go tomorrow.'

Zoe clapped her hands, hugged her dad and leapt up.

'Where are you going? You've not finished your lunch,' said Greta, but Zoe had already dashed towards the hotel. 'Going to get my hat,' she called back. 'It's hot out here.'

Zoe ran to the lift and fidgeted all the way to the tenth floor. She dived out into the hallway and checked the plant pot, but the spiders weren't there. Her stomach flipped. Where could they be? They must still be inside. She looked down at the bright orange-and-green patterned carpet and saw a small, torn piece of paper poking out from under Bradley O'Hair's office door. She picked it up then lay on the floor to look under the door.

'Milton? Audrey? Ralph? Are you there?' The gap was too small to see under. She sat up and was about to read what was on the scrap when she was suddenly aware of someone behind her.

'Miss Macey, isn't it?' It was Bradley.

Zoe gasped, stumbling to her feet and falling back into the wall.

'What exactly are you doing, young lady?' He loomed over Zoe, seeming quite big (although Dad had said he was actually only average height) and wide, and despite yet another impossibly tasteless floral shirt, he looked threatening. He fixed his little eyes on her and his mouth turned to a snarl. 'Are you spying on me?' he growled.

'I, um, I was lost,' Zoe stuttered, cringing at

the dreadful excuse. 'Your hotel is just so . . . big.' She tried a nervous smile.

Bradley leant away a little and his face relaxed. 'Well, yes, little missy. It is big. One of the biggest. Maybe *the* biggest. But still, what were you doing on the floor?'

Zoe thought quickly, surprised that her obvious flattery had worked. 'I dropped my, er, earring,' she said. 'I think it rolled under the door.'

'Uh-huh.' Bradley nodded. 'All righty, let's take a look, then. Just as long as you're not a spy. Top-secret stuff going on in here. Important stuff. Big stuff.' He slapped Zoe on the back and laughed loudly as he unlocked the door and threw it open.

Zoe crept in, watching Bradley for any clue that her suspicions were right, that he was on to her and was about to lock her in the office and she'd never be seen again. Keeping hold of the handle, she peered in and saw the spiders looking dazed on the floor. They must've been behind the door as Bradley flung it open. Zoe dashed over to them and put Ralph and Audrey in her pocket. Then she picked up Milton and whispered to him.

'Milton. I need you to hang on to my ear. Don't ask why, just do it, or we'll all be in a Hawaiian ant stew.' She stood up. 'Found it. It rolled right over here.' She lifted her hair aside to show Bradley her 'earring'.

Bradley leapt backwards like a hippopot-amus ballerina in a cartoon. 'Ugh! It's very lifelike. What is it with you and spiders?'

'Don't you like them?' asked Zoe.

'No! They're creepy and pointless and a nuisance, and they make a mess of my beautiful hotel. A lot like small girls. Now run along, little Miss Macey. And do try not to get lost up here again.' He stared at her with his cold blue eyes, then slammed the door.

CHAPTER
12
A Catastrophic Eruption

Zoe whisked them all back to her room in her hand, apart from Milton who was still clinging on to her ear for dear life. Buzzing with adrenaline, they told her what they had seen on the video – although it took an agonizingly long time on the Spida-Com – then Zoe stuck the chewed-out piece of paper into the book and wrote 'eco-crazy Maceys' next to it.

Finally, the proof they needed.

'We have to tell Dad and Greta,' she said, slamming her hand down on the bed, then snatching it back with a sharp intake of breath. But it was fine – the spiders were sitting safely on a cushion. 'Sorry, guys. I know not to do that. I'm just so angry. That awful man. Did you see his scary eyes? And the smell . . . ugh!'

The spiders mimed fainting.

'Yes, it nearly made me pass out . . . Oh – it made *you* pass out? You poor things. You are so brave. Here –' Zoe took a matchbox from her

bag – 'I saved these for you.' She tipped out a clawful of ambrosia beetles as a reward.

Ralph looked like he might be sick.

'You're the most amazing creatures, you know that? Don't you worry, Milton, we're going to get up that mountain and find your dad. And put a stop to whatever Bradley O'Scare is up to.' And with that, she popped the Do Not Disturb door hanger on the outside handle and ran to the lift.

Owen and Greta were in the lounge, huddled around Greta's laptop, up to something for sure. As soon as Zoe's dad saw her coming, he slammed the laptop shut, just like the time she'd crept up on him watching that zombie show.

'What are you doing?'

'Nothing, darling,' said Dad.

Nothing was more suspicious than 'Nothing, darling'. Zoe was now convinced that they were keeping something from her, like she was a child. Dad used to tell Zoe everything, before

Greta came along, but now it was always *them*. Like she'd been kicked out of the gang. Zoe pushed the feeling away. This was more important. She had to focus. She sat in the chair opposite, right on the edge. Her hands on her knees. 'Dad, Greta, if you can tear yourselves away from each other for one minute, something's happened.'

Dad went pale. 'Did you meet a boy?'

Zoe rolled her eyes. 'This is serious. Way more serious than boys.' She leant in. 'O'Hairy head is definitely the one bulldozing the trees and killing all the wildlife and I can pro—'

Dad interrupted her with a pointy and not very fatherly finger. 'Zoe! I've already asked you not to call him names. Let's stick to Mr O'Hair, shall we, until we've got proof . . . and after we've taken the free boat trip he's offered us.'

Zoe groaned. 'That's what I'm trying to tell you – I *have* proof.' She handed over the notebook triumphantly. Perhaps now they would listen to her.

Dad read the front cover. 'What's this?'

'Our, I mean, *my* investigation notes.'

'Why Private *Eight* Eyes?'

She looked shiftily at the floor. 'Er . . . '

Greta looked at Zoe's entries in the notebook: the clues about mud on Bradley's boots, the disregard for environmental issues and the word 'video' circled about ten times in different colours. She looked at Zoe, concern on her face and said, 'Please be careful, Zoe. Mr O'Hair is a person of interest, nothing more. Like your dad said, he's a bit different but that doesn't necessarily make him a bad guy.'

'I don't care about different – I like different, *I'm* different. But he's horrible!'

Mr Macey gasped. 'Zoe! What's got into you? Mr O'Hair has been extremely generous, we're getting this lovely hotel at a huge discount, and the spa day, and all your free movies.'

'And our boat trip,' added Greta.

Zoe rolled her eyes. 'You are both so focused

on freebies and being lovey-dovey with each other and you can't even see what's right in front of you. Bradley knows we're on to him. He's playing games with you, creating a diversion so you don't investigate him properly. Well, it's a good job we're on the case.'

'We?' said Greta. Her expression gave Zoe cause to swallow hard. Why had she been so careless and said 'we'? And with hindsight Private (Eight) Eyes was a bit obvious. She shrunk away from Greta's knowing look and turned to Dad, who seemed more interested in the spider doodles in the margins of her notebook. They were quite good, if she did say so herself. She grabbed the book and turned to the next page. 'There's the proof. Look – it's from Bradley's to-do list. Apparently all he does all day is play golf and chop down trees. He's trying to get rid of you on his silly boat, while he destroys the planet right under your noses.'

'What's going on, Zoe? This isn't like you.'

Greta took the book. 'What list? Where did you get this?'

Zoe's mouth went dry and she tried to swallow. She looked over at the bar, at the window, at the door, contemplating a quick escape, but she was trapped under their gaze.

'His office,' she said to her lap.

'His office?' Dad repeated quietly. 'What were you doing in Mr O'Hair's office?'

Zoe weighed her options. For the proof to stand up in court she'd have to tell the truth about where it came from. But at what cost? She thought of everything the spiders had gone through to get that tiny scrap of evidence to her. She couldn't let them down. It wasn't the Private (Eight) Eye way. She would have to confess.

'I was spying on him.'

Greta nodded 'Uh-huh, just you?' She ran her finger along the edge of the chewed-out scrap of paper and Zoe knew that she'd been rumbled. Her insides burnt – Greta was playing games with her, waiting for her to confess as though *she* were the criminal. It was so unfair. They stared at each other like poker players, waiting for the other to blink.

Dad came to the rescue. 'OK, Zoe Macey, PI I don't want to spoil your game, sweetheart, but I think you're taking this a bit far now.'

'It's not a game!'

'Then where's the rest of the list? Why just this little scrap? How did you even get in there?'

Zoe closed her eyes and imagined Milton's dad disappearing under the tracks of a bull-dozer. Time was ticking for him and all the happy-face spiders on the mountain and she was the only one who could save them. It didn't matter the consequences, it was time to give Greta what she wanted.

'I didn't go in.' She looked Greta in the eye and took a deep breath. 'Milton, Audrey and Ralph did. Through the keyhole. That's why it's one little chewed-out piece of a list, it's all they could carry.' Her bravery wavered as her dad stood up, spilt his drink all over his trousers and roared.

'WHAT?'

The other guests in the lounge jumped and glared at him.

Greta sighed. 'I really hoped I was wrong. Zoe, you brought your spiders on holiday, didn't you? After everything we talked about?'

Zoe shrunk into her seat but her voice was defiant. 'Milton wanted to see his dad. I couldn't leave them at home.'

Greta shook her head. 'I think you should go up to your room, Zoe.'

'Don't tell me what to do, Greta.'

'Zoe, do as Greta says,' said Dad in a small voice, running his hands through his hair.

'Why? SHE'S NOT MY MUM.'

The other guests were very pointedly *not* looking at them now, all furiously reading their books and papers, or staring out of the window at anything they could.

'Up to your room.'

'Of course you agree with her. You always take her side. Why don't you just go off and get married and forget about me? I don't know why you even brought me here.'

'Zoe—' Greta started to speak but Zoe wasn't about to be interrupted.

'You don't want me here, you're always whispering in a huddle, I should just clear off and leave you to it. It's a good job I brought my friends, at least they still appreciate me. I should go up that mountain by myself.' She snatched the notebook from the table and as the tears erupted, she ran out to the lobby and charged up the stairs to her room.

CHAPTER 13
Scruffy O'Hair

Zoe dangled her hand off the side of the catamaran over the perfectly calm, blue sea. On board, the storm was still raging between her and her 'responsible' adults, but this was Bradley O'Hair's boat, so of course it was big – big enough for her to be at one end and Dad and Greta to be at the other.

'Hey.' A shadow appeared across her arm. 'I'm Dillon.' A boy's voice.

'Who sent you? Them, or O'Hair?' Zoe didn't look up.

'No one sent me,' the boy said, sounding confused. 'And I am O'Hair. Just thought I'd say hi. I live here. I don't mean on the boat. I mean the hotel.'

'You could still be a spy.' Zoe rolled over and squinted into the sun, unable to make out his face. 'What do you mean, you're O'Hair?'

Dillon moved out of the sun, bouncing the

wide netting at the prow of the catamaran like they were on a trampoline.

She fumbled her sunglasses off, eyes wide and gripped the ropes in alarm.

He was the scruffy-haired boy in the photo – the photo that fell over during the earthquake.

'You're Dillon O'Hair?'

He posed like she was taking a picture. 'I sure am.' He had the hint of an American accent, but mixed up with something else too.

'I don't want to talk to you,' Zoe snapped and turned away folding her arms, then quickly changed her mind and grabbed the ropes again.

'There's no need to be rude. I just wanted to say hi.'

Zoe flushed, mostly with anger but with a smudge of shame too. 'I'm sorry. I don't mean to be rude really, it's just . . .'

She mentally kicked herself for almost missing the opportunity – this was Bradley's son. He could well have insider information.

'I've had a fight with my dad and his girlfriend. I'm just being grouchy. Do you want to sit?'

Dillon sat down cross-legged on the ropes. 'What did you fight about?'

Zoe thought fast. 'I wanted to go for a hike in the forest, but Dad won't let me – he says there's some building work going on and it's all closed off, but I told him you can't build stuff in the rainforest. That wouldn't be allowed because it's a nature reserve.' She watched Dillon's face closely.

He was expressionless for a moment then a smile crept across his face. 'Nicely done, Zoe Macey. I guess there's no need to pretend any more.'

'I didn't tell you my name.'

'I know who you are though. I know your dad is Owen Macey and your stepmom is Greta. You're here to stick your eco-noses in my dad's business, like that Mako dude.'

Zoe edged away from him, still clinging on to the rope netting. 'She's NOT my stepmum . . .

Are you going to throw me overboard?'

Dillon laughed loudly and a few of the other guests turned to stare at him.

'Don't be silly. What kind of person do you think I am? No, I'm supposed to keep an eye on you. Report back to Dad if you're up to anything. But I guess you're too smart for that.'

'I knew it!' exclaimed Zoe. 'Your dad knew we were coming and he's been trying to keep us away from whatever he's building on Kilauea.'

Dillon sighed. 'Why can't you just have a nice holiday, like a normal family, and keep your nose out?'

'We're not a normal family.' Zoe shrugged.

Dillon looked directly into her eyes. 'What is it about you lot and your obsession with conserving the environment? I don't get it – there's tons of environment, it's everywhere.' He swept his arm out in the direction of the vast ocean.

Could he really not know? He seemed to be genuinely asking. Zoe wondered if she could be persuasive enough to turn him. Then Dad and Greta would see how much they needed her help. 'The environment is a delicate balance. Like this boat – if it tips too far one way, we all suffer.'

Dillon *hmm*d.

'Whatever your dad is doing, he's destroying wildlife habitat. Too much habitat loss is a tipping point. There are endangered species up there that need protecting, especially the Hawaiian happy-face spiders.'

'Destroying is a strong word. He's just build-ing something to impress Mum, as usual.' Dillon looked sad for a moment. 'I never see my mum. She's always off touring the world. She's a model, actress and singer. She's amazing, so Dad is forever trying to impress her with his new projects.'

'Like dropping dry ice into the volcano from a helicopter?'

'Yeah, that wasn't one of his better ideas.' He paused. 'You're right. You're not normal are you, Zoe Macey?'

Zoe's stomach flipped, and it wasn't the boat. This was how the spider bullying had started at school last year.

'I meant it as a compliment.' Dillon smiled. 'Normal is boring. Everyone round here is sooo normal and no one really talks to me. They all think I'm spoilt 'cause I live in a mega-hotel. But I like you. Maybe you're right about this saving-the-planet stuff, but really, spiders? No one cares about spiders, do they? They're creepy. Why can't they just go somewhere else?'

Zoe risked a smile too, and wondered if she could actually turn this spider-hater into a Spider Warrior. She bounced the netting and Dillon grabbed on in surprise.

After the trip, Greta and Dad arrived at Zoe's door, armed with tea and cakes – apparently they were going to *talk*, which from the way they said it, didn't sound like a good thing to the spiders. Dad and Greta squashed on to the small sofa and Zoe sat, head down and cross-legged, on the bed with the small die-cut wooden box beside her and her toy tarantula in her lap.

She opened the box.

'You can come out now,' she said in a small voice.

Slowly, Milton, Audrey and Ralph emerged and gave half-hearted waves to the humans. Milton was glad Mini had gone to the gym – explaining another undeclared guest in the hotel might've been awkward.

'Don't blame them,' Zoe said quickly. 'It was all my idea. And I stand by it.' Her look changed to defiance. 'This is Milton's dad we're talking about. Milton's got a right to come and find him . . . we are going to find him, aren't we?'

Dad and Greta looked at each other, almost bumping noses on the cosy couch.

'I think it's time to come clean, Owen,' said Greta.

'I knew something was going on.' Zoe almost

leapt to her feet, and Milton, Audrey and Ralph grabbed the box sides, and each other.

'There's a bit more to our friendship with Mako than I let on,' said Dad.

Greta stuffed a large piece of chocolate cake into her mouth and nodded at Owen to continue.

'Thanks,' he said sarcastically. 'Greta and I have been discussing joining *#NotScaredOf-Spiders* with Mako's campaign to protect the Hawaiian happy-face spiders, and we really wanted to see the work in person. For all of us. We've been planning it for a while but we didn't want to tell you until we were sure it would work. Also, Mako and Jenna have had their eye on Bradley O'Hair for a while now. He's made quite a mess of the island, so Mako suggested we stay in his hotel to see what we could find out.'

Milton groaned. *Not the campaign again. I came here to get away from all that.*

Zoe put her head in her hands. 'So much for

this being a holiday. It's not even a rescue mission, it's a work trip. You two are spies but you still told me off for snooping! And –' she raised her voice – 'it's MY campaign.'

Milton, Audrey and Ralph gasped. They'd never seen Zoe like this before. Whatever was wrong with her? *I hope she's not going to web herself into a dark corner and refuse to come out.*

The spiders retreated into the box and Zoe hugged them close. 'Don't worry, Milton. I still care about your dad.'

14

Tremors

Dad got up from the couch and sat next to Zoe. He side-eyed the spiders in the box, still not one hundred per cent over his arachnophobia. 'I'm sorry we didn't tell you about our plans. That was a mistake. With hindsight.' He gave Greta a sheepish look and Zoe got the impression that Greta had voted for honesty from the start. 'I wanted to keep this as a holiday, especially for you. You've had a lot going on and I didn't want to worry you. I should've trusted you more.'

'We truly are sorry, Zoe,' said Greta. 'And we *are* going to find Milton's dad.'

Zoe had a sudden pang of guilt. She'd known ages ago that there might be a problem on the mountain and that Milton's dad might be involved, but she hadn't told Milton so as not to worry him. She'd done exactly what her dad and Greta had done to her.

She chewed her thumbnail. 'Let's have a look at this happy-face campaign then,' she said, eager to move on.

Dad googled it as Milton spelt out:

M Y   C O U S I N S   W I T H   D A D

'Yes,' said Greta, handing Zoe a piece of cake to make peace. 'We are planning a rescue, believe me. And we know that Bradley is trying to lure us away – he's offered us a trip around the island on the O'Hair helicopter next.'

'Ooh, I do fancy that,' said Dad, and Zoe scowled at him. 'Sorry. We've had to play along with the gifts and freebies so he didn't get suspicious. But now, with the earthquakes potentially signalling trouble, we need to move quickly – we're going up the volcano first thing tomorrow morning.'

'Thank you.' Zoe threw her arms around her dad and buried her head into his chest. 'I'm sorry I was angry.'

'I'm sorry too. Neither of us have been honest and it's not worked out so well. I'm still angry about the spiders being here, but it's done

now. It's up to you to look after them and make sure they're not discovered.'

Zoe nodded. She remembered Greta saying something about fines and serious trouble if you took non-native species abroad. She was also sure she'd used the word 'illegal', but Zoe didn't want to think about that. 'I will, Dad.'

She turned to the laptop. 'Look at these cuties, guys. If I didn't have you –' she tickled Milton's abdomen – 'they would definitely be my favourite spiders.'

Audrey and Ralph gathered round Milton as he pointed animatedly at the picture. It was a lovely photo – clearly showing the markings on the yellow abdomen, which looked exactly like a happy face, with little black eyes and a red, grinning mouth. Who would want to hurt these creatures? It was unimaginable.

But the next day things didn't quite go to plan.

'Apparently, due to the earthquakes, the two approach roads to the mountain are closed and the visitor centre is shut until further notice,' Mr M said, and without concentrating, bit into Greta's purple taro root bagel. He grimaced, but the spiders weren't sure if it was because of the news or the breakfast.

'If the roads are closed, how will we get to Dad?' Milton tapped his claws nervously and began pacing the arm of the chair.

'Have a fly, Milton, and try to calm down. They'll sort it.' Ralph handed him a snack.

Audrey abseiled from the library bookshelf and swung on to Greta's lap. She looked up at the professor and cocked her head.

'It'll be fine, Audrey. We're looking at alternative routes. There are walking trails and we've got maps and satellite views. We'll just have to go cross-country to get the footage we need to prove what a certain person is doing. I am worried, though. These road closures feel like Bradley's doing. I'm anxious about what we are getting ourselves into.'

Milton was anxious too and closed all his

eyes. He pictured his dad in the video he'd sent after the *#NotScaredOfSpiders* campaign kicked off last year. He looked so happy, so well – every bit the daring adventurer, hanging out with famous photographers in exotic locations. Now he wondered if he'd ever see his dad again. He'd spent so long without his only true family member that he'd got used to it, but here, on the island, he was so close he desperately wanted to feel his dad's eight legs around him. How could he be so near but so far away?

Milton crawled off the chair towards the dark space behind a bookshelf.

Back to those dark corners, Milton.

The thing was, of course he wanted to see his dad again, but something kept nibbling away at him.

What if Dad is disappointed in me?

Milton squeezed into the dusty gap and shuddered as a vision of a supermarket crate crept into his mind.

Most spiders ballooned off in the wind after

they emerged from their egg sac, to make a life of their own. Milton was different. He'd lived with his dad. And it had been a great life. Full of outdoor pursuits like web-rope knots and whittling splinters. They'd made dens in the garden, ignoring the garden spiders' taunts. Dad had taught him human language from the back of cereal boxes, and inspired him to always be brave and try new things.

Milton gave a half-hearted smile – *like talking to humans*.

But then his world had shed its skin. After a mishap with a supermarket delivery, Milton's dad had been whisked out into the big wide world and he'd never seen him again.

And the thing that ate Milton up from the inside was that he could've saved him.

Could I have saved him?

'So we can walk up the mountain, then?' said Zoe. Mako had joined them and Greta was showing him on the map the trail they were going to follow. 'I'm up for that.'

The adults did that annoying thing of all looking at each other, when they all had the same thing to say, but were waiting for someone else to say it first. Whatever the 'thing' was, Zoe imagined it ping-ponging around between them like a cross between a pinball and a hand grenade.

'Oh, someone say it,' she said, feeling like the only grown-up in the room.

Greta and Mako both looked at her dad and he shrunk in his chair, seeming to realize that it had to be him. 'It's just that you said "we". "*We* can walk up the mountain"...'

'Yes...'

'You can't go, sweetheart.'

'WHAT?'

'Greta and Mako are going. They're the experts. You're too young. It wouldn't be safe and I'd never forgive myself if anything happened to you. We'll stay here and eat ice cream ...' He trailed off as he saw Zoe's expression. 'Also Bradley O'Hair *has* offered us that free trip in that helicopter.'

And with that, Zoe's fury exploded.

CHAPTER 15

Things That Can't Be Unsaid

Milton's stomach churned.

He hadn't been able to face breakfast with so much on his mind. He felt dizzy again, like he had in the attic.

Find Dad, don't get squashed, climb a grumpy volcano, with Zoe probably mad at me for going without her. Some friend I am.

'Shut up!' he said aloud to the voice in his head. He was with Greta as they packed – Audrey and Ralph had stayed in Zoe's room to keep her company.

They are Zoe's real friends. They haven't aband—

'Seriously. Shut up!' Milton banged his cephalothorax with his front claws.

'Now, now, Milton. You're being too hard on yourself again.' Milton nearly jumped out of his exoskeleton. Would he ever get used to Mini's sudden appearances? 'Are you worried about Zoe being angry? She understands. It's your dad. It's why she brought you.'

'Thanks, Mini. I don't know where you've been all this time, but I'm glad you're here.'

'You ready, Milton?' called Greta, walking towards him. She held open the little wooden box and he crawled in, looking glum.

Mini crawled in after him, unseen by the relatively giant human. 'Don't worry, she'll come around. She's just upset right now.'

'I wish she were coming. She settles my nerves so much, even though she is a human. What a silly spider I am!' He smiled. 'You should swing out, Mini, you wouldn't want to get lost.'

He hugged Mini goodbye, curled up in the corner and tried to ignore the yelling coming from the neighbouring room. Mr M and Zoe were arguing, and he could guess what about. Mini popped her head back in through the holes. 'You'll be fine.'

Zoe and her dad were, indeed, arguing in Zoe's bedroom.

'It's not fair. This is my thing, the spiders are my friends, not yours or Greta's. She's got her own spiders at the zoo.' She crossed her arms again. 'She's taking over everything. First *#NotScaredOfSpiders* and now this. She didn't even want to be part of the campaign and now she's taking the credit for it – and she's got you wrapped around her little finger.'

'Now hang on, Zoe.' Her dad raised his voice, not for the first time since the others had started getting ready for the trip. 'Greta is going to be my wife, and I want you to be respectful.'

'Well, I wish she wasn't.'

It was said.

Aloud.

And despite both Zoe and her dad taking huge intakes of breath, it wouldn't go back in. Time seemed to split apart like a chasm in the Earth's crust, and all Zoe could do was watch her dad turn around and leave her room. She didn't follow, trapped by the awful thing she'd just said. She waited for the door to close behind him, then burst into tears.

Three hours later, Zoe and Dillon sat under the coconut palms on Punalu'u Beach, eating crisps. Zoe ran the black sand through her fingers. 'This is the coolest thing ever. I've never seen a completely black beach before. It's weird.'

'And hot,' said Dillon. 'It gets super hot in the sun, which is why I said to bring your sneakers. It's why the turtles like it, because it's lovely and warm.'

It was hard to be upset, watching sea turtles hauling themselves about on the beach, marvelling at handfuls of volcanic lava, cooled and

fractured by the bluest of seas. But Zoe was managing it – her face was as sullen as a rainy day in the west of England.

'What's up, Zee? Why so stressed?'

Zoe studied him – this laid-back, annoying boy, without a care in the world, or a care *for* the world. Was he still the enemy? Was she silly for thinking she could change him, trust him? She wasn't sure. She quite liked that he had a cute little name for her, though.

'Parental stuff. It's nothing.' She felt a stab of envy as she imagined Greta and Mako heading up the volcano. She pushed her palm on to the sand, letting the heat sting her skin.

'What you need is to relax, feel the sun on your face, take each day as it comes, get with the spirit of Hawaii.'

As far as Zoe was concerned there was nothing less relaxing than being told to relax.

'That's the problem. We were supposed to be relaxing. This was supposed to be a holiday.' Zoe had a sudden urge to tell someone, anyone, the whole story. 'Then I find out that Dad and Greta have been scheming behind my back about the *#NotScaredOfSpiders* campaign – MY campaign. And that's really why we're here, and then I do all the legwork working out what *your* dad is up to, with MY spiders sticking their cephalothoraxes on the line, and then they go swanning off into the sunset on a great big adventure up a volcano and leave me here with Dad, who just wants to bang on about going in a helicopter and feeding me ice cream. I'm not ten!' She beat her fists into the sand. 'And then I went and said what I said about Greta and I wish I could take it back but I . . . what?'

Dillon was frowning. 'They've gone to the volcano?'

Suddenly Zoe realized what she'd done. Cute name or not, he was still Bradley O'Hair's son, and she'd ruined everything.

CHAPTER
16
Peace Talks

In a panic, Zoe started backtracking, trying desperately to come up with a good story to cover her mistake, but for some reason Dillon was smirking. 'You should try scuba diving.'

'What? Why can't you talk sense, Dillon O'Hair?'

'You talk so much you clearly don't need to breathe.' He lay back on his beach towel. 'Don't worry, I won't say anything to Dad. In the meantime, chill out, feel the breeze, listen to the birds.'

Zoe folded her arms. 'If we don't fight for the natural world, there won't be any birds. It's your future I care about too. What your dad's doing is terrible, that's why Greta and Mako are trying to stop him. Please, will you help me?'

Dillon looked to be considering this for a moment then he said, 'It's hard for them too, you know.'

Zoe squinted at him. This habit of changing the subject was very annoying. 'What are you talking about?'

'Greta and your dad – figuring out how your family will work – it's complicated. Greta hasn't had kids before, right? She's new to it and you need to give her time. And your dad – he's trying to work out how to keep you happy and let himself be happy. He's allowed to be happy, right?'

Zoe sighed and turned her attention to two turtles playing the slowest game of tag ever. The big one in front flicked sand at the lumbering giant behind and Zoe cracked a smile. Why did Dillon have to be so frustrating? And worse still, he was right. She had been pretty awful to Greta. Of course Dad had a right to be happy. And so did she. This family thing *was* complicated, Dillon was right about that too – how irritating could one boy be?

Zoe turned to face him and gave a reluctant nod. 'Of course. But did you hear anything I said about the environment? About stopping your dad?'

'They shouldn't be going up the mountain today. Dad said it could erupt.' Dillon tilted his head and studied her thoughtfully. 'Why should I help you?'

Zoe decided to take a leap of faith. What did it matter now if he thought she was crazy? 'My spider campaign started because my best friend, Milton, was in danger. His species was under threat. And yes, he's a spider. You can laugh all you want but it's happening again, only this time it's the Hawaiian happy-face spiders and it's your dad who's going to wipe them out. We have to save them.'

Remarkably, Dillon wasn't laughing. 'I didn't

realize it was such a big deal. Dad hates bugs, so I guess he wouldn't care.' He paused. 'You really believe in your cause, don't you?'

Zoe suddenly realized how selfish she'd been. She'd made it all about her and forgotten the real goal. 'I do. Those spiders up there, and all spiders, are vitally important to the planet. But even more than that, Milton's dad is with them. Please help me save them.'

Zoe found her dad by the pool, reading a paper and drinking coffee. He didn't look cross, but Zoe's heart was hammering as she sat down on the very edge of the sun lounger beside him. Dad put down the paper and Zoe looked at him, and also the floor at the same time. She closed her eyes, expecting disappointment, feeling the heat of Dad's anger already, waiting for it to bubble up.

'Oh, Zoe. I'm so sorry,' he said.

Huh?

'I didn't realize. I mean, I didn't think. You

must be incredibly angry to say something like that.'

'I didn't mean to say it. What I mean is, I don't mean it.'

Ugh, why didn't anything come out right?

'I know, sweetheart. But you're upset and you've every right to be.'

Again, *huh*?

'Things have been hard recently, and when I met Greta, they got easier. So much easier.'

His face glowed as he spoke about her. 'But I've not paid you enough attention, or considered how you're feeling as much as I should've. Things have happened so quickly. I've been selfish.'

'It's been a bit . . . weird.'

'Yeah, I bet. I haven't tried to see things from your point of view and that's going to change. Starting now. I know how badly you want to go and rescue Milton's dad, but it's dangerous.'

Zoe looked up and raised an eyebrow.

'I know *you're* not scared, Oh Fearless One,

but I am.' They laughed. 'I don't know what's going on up there. But obviously you want to do something, so . . .'

'What?'

'We do have the helicopter ride . . .'

Zoe groaned.

'Hear me out. I know we're on the Big Island, but it's not that big. We'll get the pilot to take us over Kilauea and see what we can see from above. We might be able to get a good view of the construction work, or maybe two people hiking in the forest.'

'That's a brilliant idea! I do want to go in the helicopter – it sounds amazing fun.' Zoe paused. 'Although, it's not particularly eco-friendly, is it?'

'Neither is flying to Hawaii.'

'But we had to come to help the happy-face spiders, which is a good cause. What's the right thing to do? Use up plane fuel, but help the spiders, or stay at home and leave them?'

'That's a tough question, Zoe. You'll have to

make up your own mind about that. You can't always save the world from your laptop, though. You have to get out there and do – just ... maybe a bit closer to home next time.'

'I'm so sorry for what I said about Greta. I'm glad you're happy.'

'I know.' He gave her a big Dad-hug and Zoe felt her heart of stone melt.

CHAPTER 17

The Climb

The light changed as they went from open road to the narrow, wooded trail. Milton was glad of the shade – it was getting hot where he was. His box was in the top of Greta's rucksack, zipped under a net cover so he could see out. The sounds changed too, and that he was less glad about. Strange noises floated in from all around. Squawks and scratches, calls and crunching. Milton made himself even smaller than usual and tucked into a corner, picturing giant beaks and furry paws swooping into the top of Greta's rucksack and snatching him away.

Like Dad.

He shook the thought off and focused on the moment, but the shadows falling across his view grew larger and darker. The walls of his box felt like they were shrinking. His legs tingled and his abdomen felt two sizes too small.

In and out, Milton. Just breathe.

Slowly the world returned to normal, along with the comforting bounce of Greta's stride, and he reassured himself that, although he could see out of the bag, he was securely zipped in.

As he focused, a new sound prickled his leg hairs, something faint and far away. It sounded like Ralph's tummy, or, more like distant thunder.

I hope it's not going to rain. I thought Hawaii was supposed to be sunny. Maybe it's that global warning Zoe keeps talking about.

And then something else dawned on him. He was in the most wonderful place he had ever seen. The sounds weren't scary, they were amazing. They were bringing the magic of the rainforest right to him. He was in a forest! Exploring!

Just like D—

Suddenly the shadows in his mind lengthened again. Milton had been on his own for so long now. He was an independent spider and what if he was nothing like his dad? What if Dad was disappointed in him – a town spider? Pampered pet of humans, doing bushcraft in a downstairs loo, of all places. He only went outside to attend gala events and he couldn't remember the last time he'd attempted a lightshade to telly swing.

Of all the times I need Mini and her random words of wisdom and she's not here!

And then there was the other thought that wouldn't go away:

What if he blames me for the supermarket crate?

'STOP!'

And suddenly, as if Greta had heard him

(which was impossible), they stopped moving.

That was weird.

Greta slowly pulled her rucksack off her back and placed it on the ground. Her eyes appeared at Milton's level.

'You hear that?' she said.

Milton listened with all his leg hairs, and Mako said, 'That sounds like chainsaws to me.'

Not thunder, then.

Greta bit her lip. 'We're close.'

Milton had a lump in his throat the size of a beetle's kneecap.

The humans checked the map, pointing at places they'd marked and nodding. Milton fiddled with his claws and nibbled anxiously on the fly he'd brought with him. He knew what chainsaws were, they sounded brutal and terrifying – eating through trees like they were fly larvae. But worse still were the bulldozers – the giant earth-eaters they'd seen on Bradley's laptop. They were terrible.

*

Back down at sea level, Zoe and her dad were climbing into the O'Hair (yes, we get it, you're a billionaire) helicopter.

Zoe was trying to look as though she didn't care much for it, but her tummy was buzzing. Dad was acting like such a child and Zoe rolled her eyes as he clapped his hands and squeaked for the third time in a minute.

'This is sooo exciting!'

Fortunately, the pilot handed them all headsets to wear so Zoe was able to block out her dad. He was humming the theme tune to some ancient show he used to watch about a helicopter called Blue Chunder . . . or something.

They clambered in, fastened their seatbelts and the pilot gave them the thumbs up. Zoe didn't know what to expect when the helicopter took off, but it definitely wasn't what actually happened. At first she didn't even realize they were going. It felt a bit like the wind had caught them, then she saw that they were floating off the ground. It wasn't anything like being on the plane. There was a sort of weightlessness, then the helicopter tipped forward and they were off.

Zoe squeaked.

They could see for kilometres, and almost all around them, as the windscreen seemed to go on for ever. Zoe could see down below and out over the sea and it was all so huge and beautiful. A wave of emotion rolled up from her chest and tears pricked at her eyes.

Dad started snapping away with his camera – the cover was that he would take a ton of photos, like a regular tourist, then try to get some zoomed-in shots of the mountain.

The aircraft seemed to drift effortlessly over the bay and out across the ocean. The pilot gave them a cheeky grin, then pushed forward on the joystick and they plunged towards the sea. They both squeaked this time, and as the pilot pulled them back up again Zoe saw her chuckling to herself.

Then they were rising up and over the dark,

dense green of the rainforest, the volcano loom-
ing in the distance, long and low in front of
them. Steam rose like from a power station back
home and Zoe glanced at the pilot, suddenly
nervous. She winked and Zoe relaxed. OK,
maybe this thing wasn't going to suddenly blow
up while they were over the top of it. Dad
pointed furiously downwards at what Zoe had
thought were mudflats, except they were lumpy
and grey.

'It's lava. Solidified lava!' He was clearly
having the time of his life.

And then they were there. Kilauea was below
them, a huge pit of steam and heat. Zoe could
see orange blobs of lava, slowly rolling and
burning, but the rest of the pit looked like . . .
well, a giant cowpat. Weirdly, she wanted to go
down there and give it a stir. Except of course it
was about a thousand degrees so maybe not.

'There she is, an active volcano. Kilauea has
been erupting on and off since 1983. A lot of
steam today, though,' said the pilot.

'Is that unusual?' asked Dad.

'Hmm, much more activity than normal these past few days. But this is even more than I was expecting. The goddess of the mountain, Pele, is talking in her sleep.'

'Let's hope she doesn't wake up,' said Dad, trying to be casual.

The pilot considered the mountain for what seemed like an age, then said, 'I think it's time to turn back. Just to be on the safe side.'

Just then, Kilauea coughed and a huge bubble of bright orange lava popped violently in the crater. The helicopter pulled sharply to the left and they sped back to the airport as the pilot reported over the radio that the mountain was showing signs of life.

CHAPTER
18
The Slow and the Furious

Neither Zoe nor her dad said much after that – they were thinking the same thing: that Milton, Greta, Mako and Milton's dad were down there. And the happy-face spiders. And the rest of the island's inhabitants. What must it be like to always live in the shadow of the volcanoes?

Zoe and her dad strained to see any sign of Greta or Mako, but the forest was too thick. 'Those trails down there, are they difficult hikes?' asked Dad.

The pilot shook her head. 'Not too bad, you look fit and healthy enough. They can be a bit steep in places, but the views are amazing.'

'Shame we can't get there, what with the roads being closed,' Dad said.

'Nah, no road closures at the moment. I'd know. My wife works up at the visitor centre. But if the volcano does erupt, everything will be shut down. Your trails included.'

Zoe and her dad looked at each other. So that had been another of Bradley's diversions – he was definitely on to them. Add to that a volcano that might erupt at any moment and things were looking very bad indeed.

In the rainforest, the humans and Milton wouldn't have noticed if the volcano *was* rumbling. All they could hear was the sound of machinery.

Mako climbed down from an acacia tree, binoculars around his neck. 'It's worse than I ever imagined.' He looked distraught. 'They're clearing so much land. It's a disaster.' He rubbed the sweat from his face with a bandana. 'We need to get closer to take pictures.'

Greta picked up the rucksack. 'Are you OK, Milton?'

Milton waved his leg through the wooden box lid, as he had before, to indicate that he was fine. But of course he wasn't. He'd seen the devastation Mako was talking about, on the video. His tiny heart was hammering away. All his worrying and overthinking had been replaced by what he now realized was the truth of the matter. He was a house spider, and he wanted to go home.

They pressed on through the trees, Greta ducking under branches and stepping over rocks, then Milton heard humans shouting.

'Get down!' Mako whispered loudly.

Milton was weightless for a second as Greta dropped to the ground. His stomach plunged in slow motion and he was a little bit fly-wing sick in his mouth.

He peeked out from the box and saw it in real life – utter devastation. A huge area of land had been cleared of trees. There were tree stumps and felled trees all over the place. It looked worse than Zoe's bedroom at the weekend. There were JCBs digging up roots and dumper trucks hauling away logs. Workers swarmed about, wearing white hard hats, with a familiar logo on the front.

Bradley O'Hair.

At last the humans could see what Milton already knew. All that was left to do was take a photo, then get out of there as quickly as possible. The noise was unbearable – scraping and grinding, churning and sawing, and Milton tucked his legs under his body to muffle the sound. Why would anyone do this? How many animals' homes had been in those trees? How many spiders?

Mako's camera clicked rapidly, then he said, 'I need to get in closer. See that wooden shack over there with the cocktail bar sign on it? Head for that. There's a patch of thick cover behind it.' Milton tumbled backwards as Greta started crawling through the undergrowth.

Closer? Hang on – cocktail bar?

Zoe's dad was getting redder in the face by the minute, but apparently there were no available taxis for at least four hours. And maybe not even then. The hotel staff had clearly been told not to let them leave.

'We'll try and get a bus, or find someone in town to take us, or—'

'A golf buggy?' suggested Zoe. Joking. Definitely joking.

'That's brilliant! They're all over the place, come on.'

Zoe groaned but Dad grabbed her and pulled them into the revolving doors.

Except coming the other way was Bradley O'Hair.

Bradley stopped as the door was halfway round, bracing himself against the wall with one arm, trapping them all inside. But if they couldn't get out, then neither could he. They stared each other down, Bradley scowling at Zoe and Dad, his fingers twitching like a cowboy at high noon. Dad tutted and gave Bradley the look he used when Zoe had 'accidentally' forgotten to do her homework.

Then Zoe had an idea.

She reached into her bag for her toy tarantula and in one quick movement (so Bradley couldn't see the label and the glitter eyes and the general cuteness of it) she slammed it against the glass that separated them.

Bradley squeaked and leapt back, which in the tiny space was more of a jerky twitch, but more importantly, he let go of the wall. Dad pushed hard on their side, and the door swung round, hitting Bradley square in the bottom, sending him flying into the lobby of his own hotel, his plastic-flower *lei* flying out behind him. Looking back, Zoe saw Dillon run over to his dad and pretend to fuss over him, preventing him from standing up. He winked at Zoe before returning his overenthusiastic attention to the floundering Bradley.

Zoe mouthed a quick *thank you* at Dillon before running after her dad across the car park. They grabbed the nearest buggy, and leapt in like they were in an American cop show, burning off down the drive at a top speed of twenty-five kilometres per hour.

Milton despaired at the amount of photography Mako apparently needed to prove Bradley's guilt.

This isn't a shoot for National Geographic. *Come on!*

He buried his cephalothorax under his legs.

I'm going to be click-click-click*ing in my nightmares.*

Finally Mako was done, and with a final click, the lens cap went on the camera. Time to go. But then disaster struck. Literally. The ground shook again, and trees began whipping about violently, like a hurricane had hit. Greta and Mako fell to the ground, Greta's rucksack rolling into the mud. The diggers stopped instantly and the workers leapt from their cabs and headed in the direction of the cocktail bar shack.

Milton, Mako and Greta stared towards the mountain, their eyes widening in unison.

'THE VOLCANO!' they yelled.

And at the very same time, the noise in the trees subsided and the clearing fell silent. The workers turned towards the sound of their voices, now carrying clear across the ruined forest.

'Oi, you!' shouted a man wearing a floral hi-vis.

CHAPTER 19

Don't Worry, Be Happy

Milton rubbed his sore head. He'd been thrown from his box when Greta's rucksack fell and was now panicking under one of the straps. A gang of angry-looking workmen were heading their way and Milton felt very small and alone.

'Mini, what do I do?' Milton whispered into the breeze.

'Know when to ask for help, remember?' came the reply.

Milton looked around for his little superfan, but he couldn't see her. 'Are you actually here, or am I imagining you now? Am I going crazy?'

He clambered over the clods of earth as quickly as he could and tickled Greta's hand.

She looked down at him. 'Quick, Milton, hide!'

But Milton had a better idea. Without the Spida-Com he was voiceless to the humans, so he tried his best and pointed at himself, then out into the forest.

'Yes, Milton, go!'

He gave a broad grin and pointed to his abdomen.

Not sure if she'd understood or not, he started spinning, making just enough web to stretch to the nearest acacia tree by the time the workmen reached them. As he swung away the worker in front growled in an American drawl, 'What have we got here? Tree huggers, hey?'

From under a leaf, Milton watched as Greta stood face to face with the man. 'What you're doing here is wrong. It's illegal, it's morally disgraceful. You won't get away with it. Who do you think you are?'

'It doesn't matter who I am. It does matter who my boss is. And he's gonna squash you like bugs.' The red-faced worker turned to Mako. 'Hand it over.' He pointed at the camera.

'Not a chance,' said Mako, standing beside Greta.

'See these diggers? They can rip ancient tree roots from the ground like weeds out of . . . um . . . butter.'

Greta and Mako looked at each other.

'Yeah, so think what they'll do to you.' A JCB thundered closer, as though the point wasn't made clearly enough already.

'Hands behind your backs,' said another worker, tying their wrists with twine as the first O'Hair minion yanked the camera from around Mako's neck, catching his ear and drawing blood. He shoved them both to the ground, where they fell hard against the shack.

I guess it's up to me now.

Milton shuddered and swung away from his humans into a dense circle of forest in the middle of the site.

Owen Macey had his foot to the floor, but joggers were overtaking them.

'This is ridiculous,' he said, waving hello to a teenager on a skateboard. And it was about to get worse. From behind, the blaring honk of a car horn sounded and Zoe looked back to see a ludicrous white limousine gaining on them.

Bradley O'Hair's head appeared out of the sunroof, his yellow hair trailing behind him like a tattered flag.

'Guess Brad will be booking in another hair appointment later,' said Zoe in a brave effort to lighten the mood.

'Theft of an O'Hair golf buggy!' screeched Bradley. 'Assault of an upstanding member of the community! Smuggling dangerous animals into the country! Yes, I know about that too, little missy. You're in big trouble.'

'Dad! Do something!' yelled Zoe. 'He's getting closer!'

'Hang on to your hat!' yelled Dad. 'This is about to get real.'

Zoe grabbed the golf-buggy roof and braced herself, not sure what was worse, that Bradley would have her locked up for bringing non-native spiders to Hawaii, or the fact that Dad had just said 'about to get real'.

Dad forced the steering wheel hard to the right and they left the road, mounted the pavement and careered down a gentle slope on to the Big Beach Golf Course.

Milton swung quickly through the trees, until he reached a lush circle of ferns which seemed to be making a strange noise.

Singing?

'Because I'm happy . . .'

First I'm hearing Mini, now this.

'Clap along . . .' Milton couldn't make it out, but it was beautiful.

Following the sound, he abseiled into the foliage on a web-line, aware of a rustling in the leaves. Then, all around, he saw legs and cephalothoraxes and . . . faces! Milton gasped at the sight. *He* knew they were cousins, but out here in the rainforest, the happy-face spiders didn't have Google. Would they know he was friendly?

'I come in peace.' Milton raised a leg and looked as small and unthreatening as he could. 'Er, take me to your leader?'

'Milton?' came a voice from the back of the crowd.

He looked up as a small brown spider pushed its way to the front. 'MILTON! It *is* you! Oh, my stickiest of webs, you're really here, you found me!'

Milton felt all the air leave his book lungs. His spinnerets went dry and his legs were shaking, but there he was – a small false widow spider called Maximus.

'Dad.' Milton's voice was quiet, even for a spider the size of a tiny 'ōhelo berry.

For a moment no one moved as the spiders

regarded one another. Then, slowly, the older spider walked forward and gathered his son in his legs and hugged him with all his might.

As they let go of one another, Milton's dad turned to the gathered happy-face spiders. 'Everyone, it is my pleasure to introduce you to my son, Milton.'

A happy-face spider with a big red grin on his abdomen rushed over. 'My dear Maximus, I am happy as happy can be to meet your long-lost Milton.' And he shook Milton's front leg enthusiastically. 'I am Hau'oli, and these are

the Spinnerettes.'

Milton was engulfed by yellow. And singing!

'*Happy to see you, happy you're here, happy to meet you, happy all year.*'

'They're always singing songs about being happy,' laughed Maximus. 'Oh, Milton, I can't tell you how long I've waited for this moment.'

'Any son of Maximus is a son to us all. We're family, did you know?' Hau'oli grinned with both of his faces.

Milton nodded. 'You're a *Theridion grallator*, a relative of mine. We're both in the family *Theridiidae*.'

Hau'oli grinned. 'We're a big family and happy to welcome all. Except these humans. They are not so welcoming.'

'They're tearing down the rainforest in huge chunks. Hau'oli and the Spinnerettes here are in grave danger. The diggers are surrounding this area, and pretty soon we'll be cut off and ripped from the earth, like so many others.' Maximus shivered and Milton realized with surprise how old his dad looked.

'That's why I'm here. I've got a plan to stop them,' said Milton, looking to his dad for approval.

We haven't even had a chance to talk.

All Milton's worries about Dad being angry or disappointed in him floated away. Maximus just looked sad, and worried.

'Hauʻoli, it's wonderful to meet you, and I hope I'm not being rude, but would you mind if I had a moment with my dad. I've not seen him for such a long time and . . .' He let his words fall to the ground.

And I don't know what to say.

'We will prepare a proper Hawaiian happy-face *lūʻau* for your reunion – a traditional party – there will be much singing! You talk, be together, we're safe . . . for a while.'

Milton and Maximus found a shaded spot under a waxy green leaf.

'Milton.' Maximus stopped, as if he too couldn't quite find the words. They touched claws and then, as though this had completed some kind of circuit, they both began talking at once.

'I've missed you so much.'

'You won't believe what's been happening.'

'I'm so glad I found you.'

And then at the same time, they burst into tears.

'I'm sorry about the supermarket crate, Dad. I didn't save you.'

Maximus held Milton at leg's reach. 'Milton! It wasn't your job to save me. It was my job to protect you and I failed because of my reckless curiosity. I see you haven't been taking my advice about sticking to the dark corners.'

'I'm your son,' said Milton, wiping his eight eyes and shrugging.

'Yes, you are.' Maximus held him tight. 'I am so proud.'

CHAPTER
20
Initiation

The golf buggy tipped and lurched across the golf course, narrowly missing several sand traps, two irate golfers in pink trousers and a flock of nene geese.

'Get us off this golf course!' yelled Zoe, who was bouncing around in the back like a rodeo rider, and looking pretty sick to boot.

'There's the road,' shouted Dad. He careened around the seventh-hole flag, over a punishing patch of rough grass and, thankfully, plopped smoothly on to the slick tarmac.

And right into a traffic jam.

'This is a nightmare!' wailed Zoe. 'We'll

never reach them now.'

'We will, because we must. Greta is up there and that volcano is gearing up for an eruption.' He got out of the buggy and climbed on to the front, looking really quite heroic. Or possibly just weird.

'What are you doing?' Zoe shouted over the honking horns.

'Trying to see what's going on,' said Dad, shielding his eyes from the sun.

What was going on was that Mako's daughter, Jenna, was jogging towards them.

'Hi, Owen, why are you standing on a golf buggy? Actually, never mind, we haven't much time. A certain white limo has crashed into a JCB further up the road – he's blocking both lanes, so if you're planning on a trip up the mountain you'd better come quickly.' She pointed across the road at a white van with a WEBZ/19 News logo on the side. 'Come on, hop in. We'll take the back roads, but we'll have to be quick – Bradley O'Hair was getting back in his monstrosity of a car when I left.'

They bundled into the van, did a three-point turn, accidentally-maybe-on-purpose denting the golf buggy in the process, and sped off in the opposite direction towards the coast road.

A plan for helping Greta and Mako *and* taking out the heavy machinery was gradually forming in Milton's head, but first there had to be a sing-along, then a feast and something special that Hau'oli had promised.

'*Shiny happy spiders, holding claws,*' sang the Spinnerettes as Milton and Maximus tucked into ambrosia beetles and fire ants.

Hau'oli was explaining about the patterns on their backs. 'We're all different, but all the same. Some of us have bold markings, some none at all – we celebrate our individuality.'

'Yours are amazing,' said Milton, admiring Hau'oli's abdomen. It looked like a little clown face. Not the kind that made Zoe hide behind a cushion – this one was cute, with a big, wide smile, little black-dot eyes and arched eyebrows.

'Why do you have the faces, though?' asked Milton.

'Same as you,' said Hau'oli. 'To make others happy. Your markings are charming. The little beige face and dotty eyes. It gives me such joy to see you.'

'How can you be so happy with your home about to be destroyed?' Milton couldn't understand the spiders' permanent positivity.

'Well,' said Hau'oli, gathering the Spinnerettes to him. 'It reminds me of a song I know.'

The false widows settled down with a grasshopper smoothie to listen as the group sang about not making your troubles double by worrying about them. They all sang along with the chorus.

'*Don't worry, be happy.*'

After the singing, which included two encores and one karaoke, the happy-faces

173

suddenly fell silent and a hush spread across the ferns.

Hau'oli reared up on his hind four legs and the rest of the Spinnerettes formed a semicircle around Milton, bowing their cephalothoraxes and raising their abdomens, their happy faces surrounding him, swaying in a somewhat alarming fashion.

Milton's heart began to beat faster than the music had been.

Is this a trap? What if they're cannibals and they're going to eat me? I shouldn't speak to strange species. Why don't I ever think these things through?

The happy-face spiders drummed their claws on the ground, faster and faster, louder and louder and then Hau'oli brought his front legs down and they stopped. Silence.

Milton stopped breathing.

'*Cousin Milton, from far-off lands, brought to us by human hands—*'

They're chanting. Chanting is bad.

'*You find us in our time of need . . .*'

Here it comes, I'm going to be eaten, what rhymes with need . . .? FEED!!

'*This makes us VERY HAPPY INDEED!*'

The Spinnerettes cheered and picked Milton up on their shoulders, shouting, 'Oh, happy day!' and spinning him around. They put him down in front of Hau'oli and Maximus, who was beaming with pride and holding a tiny paintbrush made of burr bristles.

'Welcome, Milton. You are now officially a Spinnerette!' Another cheer went up as Dad painted a red smile on Milton's back in berry juice.

I'm initiated into the group! Not being made into soup.

This singing thing was catching.

CHAPTER
21
Spinnerettes Assemble!

The happy-face spiders were congratulating Milton, crowding round him and cheering, but it was being drowned out by the roar of chainsaws.

'OK, it's time to take action,' Milton shouted. 'Bradley O'Hair's gang have snared my big human friends. They came here to save you all, now we have to save them.'

'How can we do this,' asked Hau'oli, 'when we are so small?'

'We are small, but our webs are mighty,' replied Milton, remembering the incredible web displays they had made at the start of the *#NotScaredOfSpiders* campaign. 'We have powers they don't expect, and we are many. Gather together and follow me and we will show these O'Hairy people what it means to be big!'

Milton and his dad swung towards the din of the machines, with the chanting Hauʻoli and the Spinnerettes following behind. The sun was creeping down behind the mountain and the emerald green of the rainforest was giving way to shade.

Someone blew a whistle and the digger crew switched off their engines and stretched their legs.

'NOW!' called Milton.

The spiders spread out around the site, keeping under cover, then headed in groups for the vehicles and machines.

'Work fast,' Milton whispered to himself, as he clambered on to a digger.

He and Maximus slipped easily inside the bonnet. The heat was incredible, like nothing they had ever felt, not even with the radiators at home on full blast. 'Some of these parts are hotter than lava. Take care,' said Milton's dad.

Milton wiped his brow and began to spin.

Over on the back road, Jenna, Zoe and Mr Macey were making better time up the mountain, now they were in a vehicle that could actually do the speed limit.

They got as close as they could to where O'Hair's team were working, then set off along a nearby hiking trail, going downhill, which was a relief to them all, especially Jenna, who was lugging her camera.

Zoe watched Jenna, impressed that she could drive and had a real job, even if it was with her dad. As she took a moment to wonder if Greta would let her work at the zoo, fear gripped her. What if Greta was hurt or in trouble? What if she never saw Milton again? How could she have left them without saying goodbye? She'd let her anger get in the way of everything and

Greta probably thought she hated her.

Zoe hit a patch of soft leaves and slipped. Her dad grabbed her by the hand to steady her and a warm rush ran through her body. She hadn't realized how tense she was, and feeling her hand in her dad's steadied her more than physically.

'Thanks.' She looked back at him, not letting go. 'I love you.'

'I love you too, sweetheart.'

She felt suddenly overwhelmed by emotion. Not only her own, but her dad's too. It was as if it was being transmitted through her hand. His love, his pride, his desire to protect her, yet an understanding that she was quite capable, and one day, wouldn't need him so much.

She squeezed his hand. How silly – she would always need her dad. And, she realized, she needed Milton and Greta too. She desperately hoped she'd get the chance to tell them both.

No one said much. The forest was strangely

quiet and the sun was taking a relaxed ride to the horizon.

Jenna broke the silence. 'Are we going the right way? I'm not hearing construction work.'

Mr Macey looked left and right, then up through the trees. It all looked the same, which was to say, utterly different from how it'd looked from the helicopter. Then a familiar voice came squawking down the path behind them.

'Theft of my golf buggy! Assault on my delicate person! Dangerous animals!' It was Bradley O'Hair, red-faced and out of breath, huffing down the hillside towards them. 'Stop right there.'

Zoe and her dad groaned. Jenna raised the camera.

Dillon appeared from behind his dad. 'Hi, Zee!' He waved cheerily.

Owen looked at Zoe, confused. 'You know him?'

Zoe nodded, hoping that she hadn't made a

mistake trusting him.

'Right, then, Dillon. Here's how you make a citizen's arrest. Watch and learn, my son.'

'How about we arrest you, for crimes against nature?' said Owen, standing as tall as he could.

'And crimes against fashion,' muttered Jenna, adjusting her focus. 'Jenna Gonzalez, WEBZ/19 News. You're destroying the forest out here, aren't you, Mr O'Hair?'

'Definitely not.' Redness crept across Bradley's cheeks.

'Well, you are a bit, Dad,' said Dillon.

'Shush. I'm not destroying as such. Rearranging. That's all.'

'And how many endangered species have you "rearranged"?' said Jenna.

'I don't know what you mean.' Bradley pushed the camera away and started to say something, but Dillon interrupted. 'Yeah, you do. Remember when you told me that a few buggish creatures didn't matter, that the world would be better off without them, and there was loads of other green stuff to keep the tree huggers happy?'

Bradley's whole face was red now and he blustered and fumbled for words.

'Dad, they matter more than you think. You should listen to Zoe – she knows what she's talking about. There are important species up here, like the spiders. They're vital for a healthy ecosystem and they need protecting.'

'You are going to bed early tonight, young man.'

'Yeah, OK. Whatever. Look, I know the business isn't doing well, but you can't be losing *that* much. And, anyway, there are more important things than money.'

'But I'm on the verge of becoming Bradley O'Hair: Millionaire. That's what I call a disaster. I'd be . . . BOM.' He let out a little sob.

Zoe shook her head in disbelief. 'Mr O'Hair, you can't seriously think building a golf course on the side of a mountain is going to solve your business problems? It's –' she searched for a polite way to say it – 'steep.'

'But the views are spectacular.' Bradley composed himself. 'Look, how about we forget about your criminal activities for now and you all just go back to the hotel? Have a cocktail on the roof terrace, use the pool – anything.'

'Sure, we'll go. We'll just carry on our hike down the hill,' said Jenna, swinging the camera around.

'No, not that way. You can't go down there. It's top secret. Something special to get me on the front page of *House and Hotel* magazine.' Bradley dashed in front of them, reaching his hands out as wide as he could to block their path. 'In fact, you're all trespassing, so go away. Right now.'

Then from further down the track they heard shouting. A lot of shouting.

The happy-face spiders fled in all directions, web-swinging from the cabs and wheel arches, back into the trees where they clung on to the

underside of the leaves, panting, shaking, hoping they'd done enough.

Milton and Maximus fled too. They had been inside the bulldozer engine closest to where Greta and Mako were tied up, and that was where they headed.

Fury was spreading like wildfire as the construction crew tried in vain to start their engines. One leant out of the cab of his digger. 'Sir, nothing's working. What's going on?'

'I don't like it,' said another, backing away from his vehicle, looking spooked. 'It's not natural.'

'You're the ones who aren't natural!' shouted Greta. 'You tried to destroy nature. But nature is fighting back.'

The angry worker who had tied them up came at her, waving a spanner in his hands. 'Shut up, tree-hugger. Nature's no match for us. I don't know what you've done to our engines, or how you did it, but you're not so smart if you think you've stopped—'

'Er, sir?' One of the workers was leaning into a bonnet, grimacing. 'It's totally gummed up the engines.' He pulled his hand away with great strings of gluey web attached, stretching out of the vehicle like pizza cheese. 'All of them are the same. I think they're a write-off.'

Hau'oli joined Milton and Maximus and they climbed to the roof of the cocktail shack. He took a deep breath and started chanting: '*Nananana.*'

Milton and Maximus joined in.

'*Nananana, nananana, nananana . . .*'

The call spread across the rainforest, Hawaiian happy-face spiders all singing together. Other spiders joined in and before long the forest was filled with the hum, for those who had the leg hairs to hear it.

'What are we singing?' asked Milton.

'*Nananana* means spider in Hawaiian. The happy faces call themselves *nananana makaki'i* – the second word means mask. It's their call to arms.'

And with that, a swarm of spiders crawled across the forest floor and in a yellow and brown and black and white blur they made a start on chewing the ropes binding Greta and Mako's wrists.

They were just about done when Zoe, Dillon, Owen, Jenna and a frantic Bradley O'Hair came crashing into the clearing.

CHAPTER 22

Rumbled in the Jungle

There was a strange moment of silence as the new arrivals to the clearing simply stopped, frozen, mouths open. Even Bradley didn't make a sound, although Milton could practically see his brain working.

'WOW, look at this!' he stuttered. 'What a mess.' He gained confidence. 'Obviously this has nothing to do with me. My project is way further down the hill. Yes, that's it. This is someone else's terrible devastation. Nothing to do with—'

He was interrupted by the angry-looking worker. 'Sir, this isn't my fault. We've had some kind of unnatural malfunction. Caused by nature. Spiders have glued our engines up . . . with cobwebs.'

Bradley acted bemused. 'Who are you? My name is Bradley. Mr O'Hair, to you. Billionaire, if you want something. I don't know you. I'm just out for a walk with my friends.'

He slung an arm around Zoe, who squirmed out immediately, as if she'd been hugged by a giant slug, and ran as fast as she could towards the utterly out-of-place cocktail shack. 'Greta!' she yelled. 'I'm so sorry for everything terrible I said. Are you OK? Is Milton OK? I'm so, so sorry.'

Owen joined them in a tearful family embrace as Jenna filmed Mako describing the devastation around them. 'I heard of a possible environmental disaster in the rainforest of Kilauea, from my friends at the Panaewa Rainforest Zoo. Their suspicions were right – I found this construction crew destroying the forest to clear the way for a golf course.'

'A golf course? On a mountain?' Jenna panned to Bradley, who shook his head and looked unconvincingly innocent.

'As you can see, it's a terrible situation, with trees hacked down, land bulldozed and there are many protected species on these slopes, including the Hawaiian happy-face spiders.'

In response the spiders rustled the ferns, making an angry swishing sound.

Mako continued, 'I needed proof of who was responsible, and now I have it. The culprit is right here – Mr Bradley O'Hair.' Jenna turned the camera on Bradley, who was holding Dillon by his collar and shaking him.

'That's not true!' He dropped Dillon like a hot stone from the hotel spa. 'I have nothing to do with any of this. I've never seen any of these people in my life.'

Zoe put her hands on her hips. 'So why are all these workers wearing hats with your face on?'

Bradley did his best goldfish impression. 'Maybe they bought them from eBay?'

'Do we call the police?' said Owen. 'Now we have the proof we need?' He gave Zoe a thumbs-up. 'We couldn't have done this without you and the Private (Eight) Eye squad.'

Bradley threw himself to his knees and clasped his hands together, begging. 'Please, please not the police. I can't go to jail. I've seen jail cells. Even on my biggest widescreen TV they are so small. Please! I'm sorry.'

All around Milton the spiders rustled the ferns once more.

'The spiders!' exclaimed Zoe, running to the source of the movement – a yellow haze on the green leaves. 'Milton, where are you?'

A circle of yellow formed around Milton where he was sitting, alone in the middle of a fern leaf, waving with all his might. 'Zoe! I'm here,' he called, even though he knew she couldn't hear him. It didn't matter. She'd seen him and there were tears in her eyes as she reached down and stroked his abdomen.

'You're OK,' she said, with obvious relief, and carefully sat down beside him.

'How do you talk with these enormous beasts?' said Hau'oli, frustration making his happy-face shudder.

'Well, we do have to be pretty creative at times, usually in the food cupboard, and sometimes with Mr M's acrylic paints, although I wouldn't recommend it. It leaves a trail right to where you are – not good when you're trying to win a hide-and-seek championship.' Milton rolled his eyes at the memory. 'I was on for a bronze medal.' He snapped back to the moment. 'We usually use the Spida-Com, which Zoe invented.' Milton turned to Zoe and mimed typing with his legs.

She shook her head. 'We had to leave in a hurry to get here and I didn't have time to grab it.' She turned to her dad. 'How did people communicate in the old days, before computers?'

Mr M chuckled. 'The old days! We used to talk to each other instead of burying our heads in technology.' He rubbed his chin. 'Anyone know Morse code?'

Zoe looked at her dad like he was from the dark ages, but to their surprise, two hands went up. Well, one hand and one leg.

Hauʻoli arranged the Spinnerettes into a group, then stepped aside for Maximus to lead them. No one other than Hauʻoli had ever conducted the happy-face spiders, so it was an exciting moment for Milton's dad. 'I'm an explorer,' he'd explained. 'It's useful to know a quick SOS, just in case. And, of course, I'm also from the old days.' He held up his front right claw and waited for his human translator.

'Dillon, are you sure you know what you're doing?' said Zoe.

'Trust me. Like I said, I'm like you – not that normal, so I find interesting ways to entertain myself, like learning Morse code.'

Between the Spinnerettes tapping on the branches, Maximus's Morse March and Dillon's dictation they soon got Milton's message across: *Mr O'Hair. The most biggest thing is help planet. Use money for big conservation site for tourists and education. Then you famous for biggest thing ever. Saving world.*

'That is an amazing idea!' said Mako. 'What do you think, Mr O'Hair? Commit to a wonderful cause, become the world's biggest environmental sponsor?'

'Come on, Dad. Mum would be proud,' said Dillon.

Bradley chewed his lip.

'Or –' Jenna waggled the camera at him – 'I could broadcast this live on the internet. This is the sort of thing that goes viral.'

'That's blackmail.'

'It's a second chance, Bradley. We're giving you the opportunity to do something great. *Bradley O'Hair, philanthropist extraordinaire.*' Owen mimed the words as a headline in the air.

'I'll do it! I'll do whatever you want. Just don't make me wear a plain orange jumpsuit.'

Zoe approached Bradley with her hands gently cupped together. 'This is the first thing you have to do.' She knelt in front of him. 'Don't do anything silly, like screaming. They don't like it. Take a deep breath. That's it. Now say hello. Nicely.' She opened her hands and held out Milton, Maximus and Hau'oli. Bradley went white and looked at her, wide-eyed.

'This is my friend, Milton. He's big in the *#NotScaredOfSpiders* campaign. And this is Milton's dad, Maximus. He's a big adventurer. And this –' she pointed to Hau'oli – 'is one of the beautiful and endangered Hawaiian happy-face spiders that you've been terrorizing by destroying their home. I need you apologize.'

Bradley looked ill, not that anyone would notice if he was sick on his shirt, but he did as Zoe asked and took a deep breath.

'Hello, spiders.' He scrunched his face up in disgust.

'Go on,' encouraged Zoe.

'I'm sorry for chopping down your trees. It won't happen again.'

'Good,' said Zoe, popping Milton and Maximus in her pocket. 'Now, let's go back before it gets dark and have some dinner – Bradley's paying.'

'What about my guys?' said Bradley, pointing to the workers. 'I can't just send them away – they need the work.'

'Perhaps you should give them a pay rise if they agree to work on converting your golf courses into education centres.' Owen raised his eyebrows at Bradley, who nodded enthusiastically.

'Yes, yes. A big pay rise.'

Mr Angry-Looking handed Greta her rucksack, and Zoe waved to Hauʻoli as he swung back to his group.

And then the ground began to shake. More violently than ever.

The construction vehicles shuddered on their wheels and tracks, clanking and rumbling as if they had all suddenly come to life. It felt like a plane was landing in the forest.

'I'm here on the slopes of Mount Kilauea as another massive tremor hits the mountain,' Mako spoke into the camera. 'Actually, never mind . . . we need to go!' He grabbed Greta by the arm. 'Now!'

CHAPTER 23

Missing on the Mountain

'Is it erupting?' Zoe's eyes were as round as a jumping spider's.

A huge explosion shook them and they turned to see rock and ash rocketing out of the crater. Smoke was billowing out of the volcano like a runaway steam train.

All of them ran towards the track, leaping over logs and roots.

The ground continued to shake, causing the trees to twist and lean like in a storm. There was an alarming *crack* from above and a branch fell across the trail.

'That was close!' Owen grimaced, hauling it

out of the way. 'Keep a lookout above.'

Another roar came from behind them as more lava bombs were hurled into the air. The ground heaved again and they staggered this way and that. Zoe and Dillon fell forward on to the ground.

Struggling to her feet, Zoe checked her pocket. 'Milton! Maximus! Are you OK?' But her pocket was empty. 'Dad, Greta! I can't find Milton. He's gone!' She began frantically scrabbling in the undergrowth, lifting the leaves. 'I can't see him. Dad, help me.'

Owen and Greta crouched down, exchanging desperate glances. The noise from Kilauea was deafening, even though it must've been more than five kilometres away.

'Come on, there's no time,' yelled Mako. 'We must go NOW!'

Owen shook his head at Zoe. 'I'm sorry. I'm so, so sorry.'

Zoe cried out and began pushing the leaves again. 'Just a minute, I can find him, he's right here somewhere. He has to be here. I'm not leaving him.'

Her dad gripped her shoulder. 'Zoe, we have to go!'

'NO!' She twisted away, but Owen grabbed her by the armpits and pulled her up. Zoe kicked and screamed, then the ground rolled underneath them and they fell again. The sky was growing darker by the minute as the crater coughed out great lungfuls of brown ash, spraying rock and half-solidified lava like someone with a bad chest cold. 'I can't leave Milton, Dad. I won't. Don't make me.' She went limp in her dad's arms as she sobbed, tears streaking her muddied face. She knew they had to run. She would have to leave him behind.

Milton and Maximus made matching *oof* noises as they tumbled out of Zoe's pocket and rolled downhill. They came to a stop against a rotting log. Both their heads were spinning and Maximus was upside down.

Milton helped his dad to his claws, then looked around. 'Where's Zoe?'

'Yikes! She's all the way over there.' Maximus pointed back towards the trail. 'How did she fall one way and we fell the other?'

'Another downside to being small and round. Come on, let's get moving. We need to get back to her.'

They set off at a dash, but it was no good. It was like scurrying over waves as the ground rolled and pitched beneath them. They watched as Mr M got Zoe up. She was crying and shouting. Milton shouted too, then again even louder as he watched everyone fall, and stagger away down the path.

Milton looked at his dad, his eyes practically on stalks. 'She left me!'

Maximus caught up to Milton as he collapsed to the floor, clutching his cephalothorax. 'She went away. Dad! She's gone!'

'The volcano said leave. They did the right thing to listen. Don't worry, let's get help.' He cleared his throat. 'What was that song? *Na na na na na na na na . . .*'

'Dad, are you trying to call the Spinnerettes or Batman? It's this: *nananana, nananana.*'

They sang out into the forest and pretty soon a familiar yellow face appeared. Two faces, in fact.

'Hau'oli! Thank goodness you found us.'

'Why are you still here, my friends? Pele is awake, and she has a song to sing today.'

Why do they have to be so happy *all the time?*

'Hau'oli, my best friend Zoe has gone. The humans have all run away. Can you and the Spinnerettes help us get back to the town?'

'Keep singing, my friends, and all will be well.' And with that he started up the *nananana* call again, to summon his group.

It didn't take long before the Spinnerettes had gathered and Hau'oli formed them into a huddle. There was a good deal of humming and swaying, and finally Hau'oli announced that they had the solution.

'We have a party! The humans have gone. Our home is saved, so you stay here with us and be happy.'

Maximus clapped Hau'oli on the abdomen. 'I'll start catching the hors d'oeuvres.'

'NO!' Milton shouted, and the Spinnerettes stopped humming.

Hau'oli's happy face drooped. 'They're just humans.'

'They're *my* humans – my friends – and I . . . I love them. I need to get back to them.' Milton looked out across the forest, despair weaving itself across his face.

'I've got an idea,' said a tiny black spot in the air.

I'm hearing things again and now I'm seeing spots before my eyes. Unless . . .

'Mini?'

'Hi, Milton.' The tiny money spider sailed down on to the giant forest floor leaves. 'I tried to catch your eyes before, but a breeze took me. I was floating around for ages until I got snagged on that tree.'

Milton hugged her. 'I don't even want to know how you got here, but I'm very glad you are. Did you say you have a plan?'

'I have. We do what I do. We fly.'

'What do you mean, fly?' asked Milton looking unconvinced.

'We go back to the bulldozed forest and that little wooden shack. The Spinnerettes told me that the big man in the pretty shirt goes in there and makes colourful drinks with little umbrellas in. We use the umbrellas to fly over the trees and to get you home.'

'That's completely crazy!' squeaked Milton.

Almost as crazy as Bradley O'Hair drinking cocktails in the middle of the rainforest!

'Completely!' said Maximus. 'Let's do it!'

Milton had a little song of his own as they web-swung back to the clearing. It went something like this: *'We're all going to die, I don't like to fly.'* Over and over again. But everyone else was thrilled at the thought, so he had little choice but to go along with it. Besides, if it meant even a chance of getting back to Zoe, he would do it.

The Spinnerettes formed a long line and starting passing the rolled-up paper umbrellas out of the shed window and on to a high branch. It was quite a task to get them unfurled and open, but working together in harmony, they got it done. Spiders were allocated, four to an umbrella, and Milton, Maximus, Hauʻoli and Mini all held on tightly as they angled their umbrella to the wind.

'Do you remember when I brought you to live with me?' called Maximus over the breeze. 'You ballooned right into a rose bush!'

Milton groaned. 'Well, let's hope this goes a bit better.' He was mid-eye-roll at his dad when the wind caught them, and they were off.

Milton's stomach lurched as they rose, then dipped sharply as the breeze dropped. They fell swiftly towards the treetops, Milton screaming, his dad laughing, and then the wind caught them again and they headed away from the crater and towards the sea.

THE SEA?

Little spots danced in front of Milton's eyes and his grip loosened on the cocktail-stick umbrella handle.

'Milton!' His dad grabbed him and shook him hard. 'Don't pass out, you're missing the best bit – look.' He pointed, and Milton saw all the other little umbrellas, bouncing and dancing behind them like candy-coloured butterflies.

Milton tried to calm his breathing and focus on holding on tightly. He made an effort to remember everything – One Short would love this, and he was determined to last long enough to tell her all about it when they got home.

Home. I do want to go home. I'm not my father's son after all. I'm not an adventurer, and that's OK.

'Time to angle,' yelled Hau'oli, and they tipped themselves towards the ground. 'We're

aiming for that big green space down there. Nice and flat and perfect for a landing. Spiders, prepare for final approach.'

Bruised and shaken, the humans made it back to the main road and got a lift into town.

No one spoke as the pickup truck they'd ridden in pulled up beside the O'Hair Hula Hole Golf Course to drop off Mako and Jenna. The only sound was Zoe's breath as it caught in her chest – she was all out of tears.

'What on earth . . .?' said Dillon, pulling a weird face. 'Guys, come and look at this.'

Everyone got out of the car and looked to where Dillon was pointing – except Zoe, who carried on looking at her shoes.

'What is it?' Bradley hid behind Greta. 'A swarm of hideous yet colourful creepy-crawlies?' He flapped his arms, readying himself to swat them away.

'Nope. Flying cocktail umbrellas,' said Jenna. 'And they're heading for the fairway.'

The umbrellas got lower and lower and then a series of tiny yellow (and three brown) skydivers launched from the handles, floating down to earth on their webs. The umbrellas plopped on to the ground around them, the cocktail sticks spiking into the grass.

'Spiders!' squeaked Bradley, and Zoe's head flicked up.

'Where?' she gasped, then seeing the array of tiny parasols she ran across the grass and lay on her tummy to get a better look. Her eyes darted from one yellow happy face to another until . . . there he was.

Milton.

Tears flooded from her eyes, and his, and she held her hands out to him. 'I thought I'd lost you for ever. I'm so sorry I left you. I'll never leave you alone again.'

Milton wiped his eyes and made the tiniest little heart shape with his claws.

Zoe sobbed. 'I love you too.'

CHAPTER
24
Beach Buggy

Two days later and halfway through a dream about surfing on a turtle, Zoe was awoken by a hammering at her door.

Through the spyhole she saw the forest-like top of Dillon's hair.

'What do you want?' She let him in. 'It's early.'

'You're a scary-looking creature in the morning, Zoe Macey.' He smiled, then quickly put on a look of concern. 'I came here to tell you to get dressed quickly. Something has happened on the beach and your dad wants you right away.'

Zoe raised an eyebrow. 'What's happened? Why is Dad up so early?'

'I don't know.' Dillon grabbed her shoulders. 'But he looked pretty frantic. You should do as he says.' He spun her around towards the bathroom.

Zoe shuffled to the door, grabbing a pair of shorts and a T-shirt from the end of the bed as she went.

'And brush your teeth,' Dillon called after her.

Zoe ran her hands through her hair as she returned to the bedroom, only then realizing that Dillon was still hanging around.

'Come on, come on,' he said, hopping from one foot to the other.

Zoe paused to size him up. Something was weird about this whole situa—

Dillon grabbed her arm, dragged her out of her room and along the corridor to the lifts.

As the doors closed and he pressed the button for the ground floor, his willpower seemed to leave him and he broke into a wide grin.

Zoe shifted her weight, her hands finding their usual spot on her hips. 'What?'

'I can't. I mean . . .' He tried to rearrange his face back to its previous look of poorly-acted concern. 'Something big is going on.'

The lift doors opened and Dillon grabbed her again, pulling her through the lobby and out of the revolving doors.

'Ta-da!' Dillon gestured to the waiting golf buggy with a flourish. 'Your carriage awaits, my lady.' He put a brightly coloured hibiscus *lei* over her head and ushered her into the back seats before climbing in after her.

As they pootled along the street towards the beach, Dillon refused to answer any of Zoe's questions, repeatedly making an annoying lips-zipped motion every time she asked. So she gave up and folded her arms, almost crushing the flowers.

Not long after (although long enough at only twenty-five kilometres per hour) they were welcomed by a queue of people clapping and smiling.

A Hawaiian woman, dressed in the most beautiful flower headdress took her hand. 'Our VIP guest has arrived. Zoe, please come with me. Your dad and Greta are waiting for you.'

Confusion rippled across Zoe's face, as she walked along the queue of people, all smiling at her. Bradley and what looked like the entire hotel staff were there, and the lady from the ice-cream shop. Jenna and Mako were a bit further along, though not filming thankfully. Jenna did have a normal camera, though, and was taking pictures.

What on earth was going on?

At the end of the queue, two people were holding enormous palm leaves across her path, blocking her view of the sea. As she approached they pulled them back with a dramatic flourish, to reveal the scene on the beach.

There was her dad, beaming at her with a smile that seemed to reach right down to his feet. Further down the beach, wearing an incredible flowing white dress, was Greta.

'Dad?' Zoe took her dad's arm, still processing what was happening.

'Zoe, sweetheart. You are our most important guest – Maid of Honour and Best Girl all in one. Without you I would never have met Greta. You brought us together, and now would you do me the incredible honour of giving me away?'

Zoe's mouth fell open. 'What do I do?'

'Just say yes.'

'OK. I mean, yes!' Happiness washed over her in waves. 'You're getting married? Here? Now?' She hugged her dad almost violently.

'We are now you're here. So mind the threads.' Owen smoothed his jacket.

'Oh, Dad, you are so uncool. But this is the coolest thing ever.' She linked her arm in his.

'Come on, then, let's not keep the bride waiting. She might think you're about to do a runner in a golf buggy.'

CHAPTER 25

Hawaiian Happy Family

The ceremony was perfect – even the spiders, who had never attended a human wedding before (or any wedding, come to that) were overcome with emotion. With so many eyes to cry with they had created a small puddle between them.

'Oh, that was so beautiful,' wailed Ralph.

'Look at them all, dancing together. Doesn't Zoe look happy in between her dad and Greta?' Milton sighed contentedly. 'I think she's found her place in the family.'

But Ralph and Audrey weren't listening. They were dancing too, Ralph spinning Audrey beneath his large hairy legs.

Maximus wandered over to Milton and stretched out under one of the human's parasols. 'This heat is too much for me, son. I preferred it under the canopy of the trees.'

Milton looked up. The umbrella was somewhat bigger than the one they had soared through the air on. It made his tummy flip to think of it and, now he'd survived in one piece, for some reason he couldn't help going over all

the terrible things that could've happened. Mainly involving birds. He resolved to live a much more boring life in future and be grateful for everything he had back at home.

'Still buzzing from our wild ride?' said his dad. Maximus looked pleased with himself, but in the light Milton noticed how grey his abdomen was getting and as he reached for a caterpillar kebab he looked stiff in the legs, slower than Milton had realized.

Maximus took a long, refreshing drink of Hawaiian blue lady beetle juice. 'So, Milton, serious question time. What do you think of Hauʻoli's suggestion? You like it here, right?'

Milton gazed across the black beach to the sea and breathed in the clear air. 'It's pretty, and warm. I like that.'

'Sure, and the food's good, right?' He sucked ambrosia-beetle dip from his claw. 'So, how about it? You want to stay? Live out here with your old dad? My human's sticking around for a while, then who knows? He's such an adventurer is Mako, never a dull moment with him. Africa, Australia, Antarctica? It's a heck of a life.'

Ralph froze in the middle of an Audrey-twirl and her legs twisted like a rope so she fell over sideways. They both took a deep breath as Milton stumbled over an answer.

Don't make me choose, please. That's not fair.

'Your friends can stay too, of course,' said Maximus.

'I thought you'd be coming home with us,' said Milton. 'And Zoe and Mr M. I mean, Hawaii is lovely, but if this is what a holiday's like I plan to go home and never leave again.'

Audrey's legs un-twizzled.

'And miss all this? Milton, I haven't even done that volcano swing yet. It's my life's ambition and it's so close. Especially since it was only a minor eruption – just a false alarm, really.'

'Mr Milton,' said Ralph. 'I'm not the hairiest spider in the box –' The others gave him a baffled look – he absolutely *was* the hairiest spider in the box – 'but I'm pretty sure a volcano is too hot to swing across.' He looked at Audrey for confirmation. 'It's a hot thing, right?'

Audrey and Milton nodded.

'Dad, you're a spider of the world. You must know you can't swing over a pit of molten lava.'

Maximus shuffled his claws. 'What about a hot vent? A little crack with some steam coming up . . .' He crumpled on the table. 'Truth is, Milton. I think I'm on my last legs. I just thought, if I could do one more big swing.'

'Our new house is quite big,' said Milton gently. 'The TV is *very* far away from the lightshade now. I mean, it's a really long swing. I've tried, but I can't do it.'

Maximus sighed, though there was a tiny glimmer in his eyes. 'If you'll have me . . . I'll pack my bags. UK, here I come.'

Jenna and Mako came over with Zoe and took some pictures of all the arachnids.

'I'm going to squeeze in a quick interview with Mr O'Hair for WEBZ/19 News about his amazing conversion to the environmental cause. Zoe, could you bring Milton over for a picture? It was his idea after all.'

Zoe crouched down to Milton, who was shaking his head violently. 'Would you like to come with me and be on telly again?'

NO THANKS
I HAD ENOUGH BEING FAMOUS

'I understand. It's probably for the best anyway. Bradley said something about hiring you as his project manager.' She rolled her eyes. 'And we thought a mountainside golf course was ridiculous. Stay under the shade with my dad. I think he's had a bit much sun, and one too many slices of wedding cake!'

'Have you really had enough of fame?' asked Audrey.

'Fame is a funny thing, but I think I've figured it out. I can do good and be famous, without being a celebrity. I don't need the charity records and sportswear endorsements. I just need to be myself and be with you guys and live in the attic and catch flies for my family.'

'You're not giving up on the campaign, are you?' said Ralph.

'Not at all. *#NotScaredOfSpiders* is more important than ever, and I'm going to be supporting the work here and at home.' He put a leg around Mini's shoulder. 'And I have my new personal assistant here, who's going to help me manage my work/life balance.' Mini gave Milton the tiniest of tiny high-ones. 'But I'm a spider and it's OK to keep—'

Ralph nodded sagely. 'To dark corners, right?'

'Not quite. I was going to say, keep my eight feet on the ground.'

It was a wonderful end to the holiday, but an end it was, and after some tearful goodbyes (Bradley went through three, increasingly hideous, hankies) they set off for the airport, their stowaways all safely hidden away. The trip home seemed longer than on the way out and Zoe was more exhausted than ever. She spent most of the flight with her head on Greta's lap, snoozing. Five spiders safely tucked inside their box.

There were no pat downs, no limousines, no one waiting to collect them. Just a quiet ride home and their old familiar front door.

Zoe took a deep breath as she went into the hall, the spiders riding on her forearm. It smelt of home . . . and a little bit like old rubbish.

'Owen, did you empty the bin before we left?' said Greta.

Zoe's dad made a can-I-quickly-go-back-in-time-and-do-that-now? face and dashed back out to get the rest of the suitcases.

'Let's have a cup of tea,' said Greta to Zoe as she went into the kitchen.

'Sit down, Greta. I'll make it for you.' And she hugged her stepmum. 'Thank you for a great holiday. I know it was a bit crazy, but I'm glad we were all together.'

Greta gave her a big squeeze. 'And I'm glad that Kilauea didn't completely blow its top. That wouldn't have got me many new-parent points!'

'You're doing OK. I'll let you off,' said Zoe as she put the kettle on and laughed at her dad, who was tying the top of the three-week-old bin bag with his jumper over his nose.

While the kettle boiled, Zoe opened her laptop, and Milton, Maximus, Audrey, Ralph and Mini eyed up the dusty shelves for something to eat.

'Can't you leave that alone for five minutes?' scolded Owen, rolling his eyes.

'I've left it alone for hours – a whole day has passed, and don't blame the time zones. Ooh, look at this – what a nice write-up.'

On-screen was a newspaper article from the *Big Hawaii Post*, about the remarkable environmental plans being revealed by local billionaire, Mr Bradley O'Hair. On the front cover was a big photo of Bradley and Dillon, and in a side box, pictures of Milton, Hau'oli and the Spinnerettes.

The spiders all turned nervously to look at Milton as if he were about to break, or explode, or run away again. But he simply nodded and Zoe grabbed the Spida-Com.

WE DID A GOOD THING

Then he looked at the others and pointed to the stairs.

'Yes, you go off and get settled in,' said Zoe.

YOU TOO

he typed, as Zoe and her parents had a family hug.

Milton's claws were shaking a little as he showed his dad up the stairs, through the hatch and under the beam in the attic. For the longest time he'd wanted his dad to come home, and now he had, Milton was nervous. This was his life, and it was very different from his dad's. Certainly there were fewer opportunities for natural disasters. Would Dad be disappointed?

Lost in thought, he didn't notice One Short bombing towards them. 'You're home! I missed you.'

'One Short, I'd like you meet my dad, Maximus. Dad, this is our friend, One Short.'

'A garden spider?' Maximus hung back.

'Yes, it's a long story,' said Ralph. 'I'll tell you all about it.'

They all chuckled.

'So . . . what do you think?' asked Milton nervously.

Maximus smiled. 'I think it looks like home.'

What Happened Next . . .

Bradley O'Hair was as good as his word and opened a top-class environmental education centre on the Big Island. The clearing was replanted and Bradley also donated one of his golf courses to become a nature reserve. Just one, so far, but Mako and Jenna are working on him.

Maximus reclaimed his position as champion of the lightshade to telly swing. Try as he might, Milton can't quite beat him.

The *#NotScaredOfSpiders* campaign launched a new Hawaiian happy-face line of merchandise, including T-shirts and baseball caps. Dillon has one in every colour available.

Zoe, Owen and Greta all went on holiday again, this time camping. In Wales. Nothing whatsoever happened, and it was perfect.

The End

More Spidery Sciencey Stuff

Meet Milton's newest friends – the Hawaiian happy-face spider and the money spider are, of course, both real spider species. Money spiders make up the largest group of spiders in the world with Mini's species being the most common in the UK. On the other hand Hauʻoli and his friends are under threat and their numbers are reducing due to habitat loss and predation (that is to say being eaten).

Hauʻoli – *Theridion grallator*

The Hawaiian happy-face spider is found naturally on only four of the Hawaiian Islands. They are small, like Milton, and very hard to spot as they spend much of their time hiding under forest leaves.

It's not known why they have such unusual markings, but they are all different; some smile, some frown, some don't have faces at all (maybe they're just shy?).

They are generally found high up in the rain-forest, where they are less likely to be eaten by the many non-native species in Hawaii.

Mini – *Lepthyphantes tenuis*
Mini is from a family of spiders called *Liny-phiidae*, so you could call her 'Mini the Liny'.

Around a third of all spiders in the UK are money spiders, and are said to bring good fortune if they run on your clothes.

They build delicate sheet webs, sometimes seen on frosty mornings covering fields, and can travel hundreds of kilometres on their thin strands of web.

New species of money spider are being discovered all the time!

'Don't Worry, We're Just Spiders' by Hau'oli and the Spinnerettes

Here's a little song we wrote,
If you love spiders, you should take note.
We're not creepy,
We're just crawly.

We love the mossies and we love the flies,
And especially centipede surprise.
We're not scary,
We're just hairy.

So don't you smash us or squash us, please,
It's really tough on our forty-eight knees.
We're not huggy (sorry, we like our personal
    space),
We're just buggy.

(Ooh, ooh ooh ooh oo-ooh ooh oo-ooh) we're
    not bitey,
(Ooh, ooh ooh ooh oo-ooh ooh oo-ooh) we're
    just mighty.
(Ooh, ooh ooh ooh oo-ooh ooh oo-ooh) don't
    worry, we're just spiders.

References to the original song 'Don't Worry, Be Happy' by Bobby
McFerrin were approved by him.

A Lot (More) to be Thankful For . . .

Sitting down to write the sequel to *Milton the Mighty* was daunting at first, but turned out to be enormous fun. Not only could I return to my favourite eight-legged buddies, meet some new ones, and reimagine songs for the Spinnerettes, but also I got to work with my favourite people all over again. As ever, I am indebted to them for their support, knowledge, guidance and gifs.

Thank you, Chicken House, it's truly an honour and I'm still pinching myself even though we're on book two.

Lauren, my stellar agent, I am so grateful for your support and for being Spider Warrior-in-Chief.

Group-hug gifs go out to The Web People. Spider silk is stronger than steel and so are we.

And too many other amazing writing friends to mention by name (Emma A, Swaggers gonna

Swag, WriteMentor, SCBWI, Bath Novel Award . . .)

It's been a privilege to be involved with Bath Libraries (and spend time with wonderful librarians, especially Louise Judge), BOAMBF, Bath Children's Literature Festival, Bristol Storytale Festival and some incredible indie bookshops: Mr B's Emporium, Storysmith, Tales on Moon Lane and Max Minerva's. Thank you also to Buglife and BAS for their support. Join the Bug Club at: www.amentsoc.org/bug-club/

I'd like to raise a glass of ladybird juice to all the people volunteering at Community Libraries across the country, and also to Stuart White – people who give back to the world in a most wonderfully bookish way.

Thank you to all the readers – Spider Warriors all, to my Spiderlings for not being embarrassed of me (yet) and to James for pretty much everything.